**"I ... Dean ... I'm really not ..."
Jennie gasped and drew away.**

"I think you are," Dean said. "I think we both are. He took her hands in his. "I knew this was right more than a year ago."

She gave him a lopsided smile. "Well, in that case you're a pretty slow study."

"You're right. Frankly, lady, I'm shy."

"But why is this happening to us now?" Jennie persisted softly. She could feel it from him, too, a growing flame that licked at the two of them.

"We both opened our eyes at the same time, I suppose. I held off too long, too long." His fingers traced the contours of her face, memorizing each facet of it. So lovely, so willing ...

Petra Diamond writes her romances in a large Victorian house in New Jersey in the company of her baby daughter, her author husband, three cats, and a dog. A former actress and hardcover book editor, Petra has been writing full-time for the past five years. She has published both teen and adult romances, educational screenplays, and nonfiction books on a variety of subjects.

Dear Reader:

The lazy days of summer are here, a perfect time to enjoy July's SECOND CHANCE AT LOVE romances.

In *Master Touch* (#274) Jasmine Craig reintroduces Hollywood idol Damion Tanner, who you'll remember as Lynn Frampton's boss in *Dear Adam* (#243). Damion *looks* like a typical devastating womanizer, but inside he's a man of intriguing depth, complexity, and contradictory impulses. He dislikes Alessandra Hawkins on sight, but can't resist pursuing her. Alessandra is thoroughly disdainful of Damion, and equally smitten. You'll love reading how these two marvelously antagonistic characters walk backward into love — resisting all the way!

In *Night of a Thousand Stars* (#275) Petra Diamond takes you where no couple has gone before — to sex in space! Astronaut Jennie Jacobs and ace pilot Dean Bradshaw have *all* the "right stuff" for such an experiment, but they've had little time to explore their more tender feelings. Suddenly their emotions catch up with them, making their coming together a bristly, challenging proposition. Petra Diamond handles their love story with sensitive realism, making *Night of a Thousand Stars* out of this world.

Laine Allen, an exciting newcomer, turns romance stereotypes on their heads in *Undercover Kisses* (#276). Every time private eye Katrina Langley asks herself, "How wrong could a woman be about a man," ultra-manly Moss Adams suggests the answer: "Very wrong!" Every time Kat thinks they're evenly matched, Moss cheerfully knocks her off balance. Moss's intelligent deviltry and Kat's swift-witted ripostes will keep you chuckling as you discover the secrets they keep from each other, while unraveling a most perplexing intrigue.

SECOND CHANCE AT LOVE is pleased to introduce another new writer — Elizabeth Henry, author of *Man Trouble* (#277). Like other heroines you've met, Marcy has a low opinion of men — especially Rick Davenport, who climbs through her bedroom window after midnight and challenges her to all sorts of fun and games. But no other heroine must contend with an alter ego called Nosy, who butts in with unasked-for advice. Nonstop banter makes *Man Trouble* as light, crunchy, and fun to consume as popcorn.

In *Suddenly That Summer* (#278) by Jennifer Rose, Carrie Delaney's so fed up with the dating game that she spends a week at a tacky singles resort, determined to find a husband. But she's so busy participating in the toga party, forest scavenger hunt, and after-dark skinny dip that she refuses to recognize the man of her dreams — even when he insists he's "it"! Thank goodness James Luddington has the cleverness and persistence to win Carrie by fair means or foul. Finding a mate has never been so confusing — or so much fun!

In *Sweet Enchantment* (#279), Diana Mars employs warmth and skill to convey the joys and heartaches of combining two families into one through a new marriage. Pamela Shaw, whom you know as Barrett Shaw's sister-in-law in *Sweet Trespass* (#182), has to deal with her son's antagonism toward her new love, Grady Talliver, *and* with Grady's four young sons. But lizards in the bathroom, a bed sprayed with perfume, and a chamber of horrors in the attic don't ruffle our heroine, who more than adequately turns the tables on her little darlings. *Sweet Enchantment* is a story many of you will identify with — and all of you will enjoy.

Have fun!

Ellen Edwards

Ellen Edwards, Senior Editor
SECOND CHANCE AT LOVE
The Berkley Publishing Group
200 Madison Avenue
New York, N.Y. 10016

Second Chance at Love

NIGHT OF
A THOUSAND STARS
PETRA DIAMOND

A
SECOND CHANCE AT LOVE
BOOK

NIGHT OF A THOUSAND STARS

Requests for permission to make copies of any part of the work should be mailed to: Permissions, Second Chance at Love, The Berkley Publishing Group, 200 Madison Avenue, New York, NY 10016.

First edition published July 1985

First printing

"Second Chance at Love" and the butterfly emblem are trademarks belonging to Jove Publications, Inc.

Printed in the United States of America

Second Chance at Love books are published by
The Berkley Publishing Group
200 Madison Avenue, New York, NY 10016

Acknowledgments

My sincere thanks to the National Aeronautics and Space Administration, and particularly to Steve Nesbitt and Frank Hughes, for their generous time and invaluable assistance.

- *Prologue* -

"OKAY, NEXT UP! JACOBS!"

Jennie stepped out into space, her feet leaving the platform, her head coming up as she had been taught. The facility at Vance Air Force Base in Enid, Oklahoma, was the highest one NASA had, which meant that everyone got shipped out here at some point for parachute training.

The chute was rigged and extended at the apex of the high tower, but even so, you still felt as if you were falling off the top of the world. Jennie held on to the straps of her harness and started sailing, remembering not to look down. The smile on her face was a little forced—but, after all, nobody really *relished* this exercise. It was just another fun event in the always exciting life of an astronaut. No matter what some of the other clowns in training said about hanging their rears off the edge, the guys were just as nervous about this part as the women.

Now! she thought as her body passed the second level of the tower. The static line pulled and held. The apparatus tightened with a pop around her already sore shoulders, and she winced as she pulled back on the

1

straps for some counterpressure. If only Andy could see her now! When her husband was alive, they used to try to fly each other out of the skies, their two Cessnas dipping and chasing like sparrows playing a game. But parachuting—he never would have believed Jennie had the guts. Although maybe it wasn't just guts. Maybe it was dumbs.

Why are any of us nuts enough to make a living like this? she reflected just as she heard a strange vibration above her. And before she could even begin to question what it was, she stopped dead in space, some thousand yards above the earth. There she was, stuck in midair.

Oh, no! she thought miserably. Now I have to do it again! NASA's no-nonsense training policy was that astronauts repeated a procedure over and over until they could do it in their sleep, whether it was handle a press conference or take a turn in the centrifuge machine. If there was anything Jennie hated more than parachuting, she couldn't name it.

She kicked out, wondering what she had messed up this time. But she wouldn't budge; she was caught like a bug on a pin. And what was worse, two of the suspension lines had broken. One was wound around her leg; the other held her left arm flat against the tower.

"Hey, Jacobs, you trying to fly?" she heard her immediate commander, Captain Steve Akins, shout down to her.

"No, just taking a rest," she called back, attempting to sound cool as ice.

"Hey, move it, will ya? The rest of us want a turn." That deep baritone voice came from Dean Bradshaw, fearless ace flyer and the envy of all, since he was probably the next good doobie to go up. *His* flight selection was practically guaranteed, dammit.

"Gee, Dean, I kinda like it down here. Guess I'll stay awhile!" Jennie yelled. Frankly, she was as embarrassed as she'd ever been. One astronaut messing up meant everyone else had to wait and lose precious time on the apparatus. But she saw no way to cut herself loose in her present position. Her right arm was too far away to reach the knife slung low on her belt, and her left arm was pinned in an upright position. And both were starting to hurt—a lot.

"Get her down, Bradshaw. Damn women!" Steve Akins was clearly exasperated with this hiatus in his carefully planned day.

Jennie had no choice. There was nothing to do but dangle there, half against the tower, half hanging in midair, and wait to be rescued. It really burned her up, relying on someone else to get her out of a mess. And it *would* have to be Dean Bradshaw. Since mission specialists and pilots trained separately for the most part, she hardly knew the man, except by sight—who could miss the handsome devil?—and by reputation—he was one of those flyers who could do no wrong.

"Well, hurry up, for heaven's sake!" she told Bradshaw when the crane he was riding came within talking distance. NASA provided a special truck for occasions like this. Everyone who had to use its special services got a big demerit, right on the record.

"You look so pretty up there, lady, like a bird in a tree. I just can't bring myself to ruin the picture."

"All right, wise guy, I've had enough." Jennie felt herself beginning to sweat. Her arms were on fire now, and her tied-up leg was asleep. And here was this steely-eyed space eagle, Dean Bradshaw, who was never sick, never defeated, never too tired to try a maneuver again. This guy couldn't only fly any plane NASA threw at him—he could fly the box it came in! Just looking into his midnight-blue eyes and watching the grin on his raw-boned, angular face made her grit her teeth. He was so nonchalant about everything, and everything came easy to him. You could bet this guy didn't have any demerits—no, sir, no way.

Then she felt his powerful arms wrap around her hips, lifting her as he reached for the harness. He tried to unhook it from the tower, but the lines above it were shredded, tied tightly around the metal poles.

"Got to use a knife, lady. You afraid of blood?"

"Only yours, cowboy," she joked, pretending the pain had gone away. There was another feeling, though, beyond the pain. Something she hadn't felt for years. What was it? She looked down into his rugged face, and the earth rushed up toward her. Suddenly, she was dizzy.

She felt him sawing away at the straps and gripped his broad shoulders hard, making her muscles relax as much as she could. And still she smiled. Wouldn't Andy be proud of her now! As the last line came free, she slipped down several notches and gasped when Dean caught her again, pulling her close. She had no choice but to wrap her legs around him and let his weight carry her. But he didn't move.

"Well, mission accomplished, cowboy. Let's get a move on." Jenny knew everyone was watching them, and that was a worse pain than the one in her arms. It didn't help matters any that she could hear the spectators around them chuckling.

"Just a second. I'm getting my bearings." His face was so close she had to tilt her head back so as not to touch it. That body plastered against hers was as solid as rock, but certain parts of it were harder than others. This was terrible and, what was worse, completely uncalled for in the NASA rule book.

"Dammit, Bradshaw, let me onto that crane." She was annoyed by her own reaction. There was no need to feel like a blushing schoolgirl just because this infuriatingly attractive guy had her in a half-Nelson.

"I'm kind of enjoying this part." He hitched one arm up higher, and the nylon of her jumpsuit smoothed out against the rounded curves of her breasts. He was staring right at them, right though the material.

"I've never seen anyone manage this maneuver quite this way," he said, slowly letting his tongue run around the perimeter of his wide, sensual mouth. "Mind telling me how you did it?"

Jennie heard the laughter below them get louder.

"It was exceptionally difficult. I practice on the tree in my backyard. Bradshaw, please!" She could hardly bear his blue eyes on her, so personal and so piercing. It was as if he'd stripped her of all her emotional armor— as well as her clothing. And he wouldn't stop staring! "Look, mister, I want down, and I mean now."

"Is that a nice attitude to have when someone's trying to help you?" At her glare, he shrugged and added, "Okay for you." Then he dropped her, and she landed with an awkward plop on the top deck of the truck, her feet smarting, her face burning. Everyone—astronauts, trainers, and ground crew included—was in hysterics. They all got such a kick out of practical jokes around here.

With as much dignity as she could muster, Jennie clambered down the rest of the steps and jumped to the ground. She didn't turn around once because she knew that if she had, Dean Bradshaw would have been standing there with his damned huge hands on his damned small hips, loving every minute of it.

Well, he might be Mr. Wonderful to everyone else, but he certainly wasn't to her. And he might be waltzing his way onto the next space shuttle, but Jennie was determined that she was going to work hard enough to get her own day in the sun—or on the moon, one or the other.

- 1 -

Nasa Road 1 led in a straight path right to the Johnson Space Center, located in the heart of Clear Lake City, just outside Houston. Leave it to the optimists of space to call it that—the complex had been built on the flats near the muddy shore of this ugly puddle, and there was nothing remotely clear about it. Funny, though, as soon as you were tapped to become an astronaut, things started looking rosy to you—even mud puddles.

As Jennie Jacobs pulled out of her reserved space in Parking Lot 2, she thought about her first day here, over three years ago now. What a stupid rookie she'd been, so thrilled to have been winnowed out from that group of over five thousand applicants that she would have bet she could make Mach 1 without a plane. It wasn't any great honor, as Andy told her later. Hell, they could spot and eliminate the lunatic fringe among candidates in a minute—the I-want-to-be-an-astronaut-so-I-can-go-live-on-Mars type—and real credentials were easy enough to validate.

Jennie had the "right stuff" as far as any of that was concerned. As her NASA application clearly showed, she was no slouch at life, nor did she have any intention of letting a thing slip by her. At thirty-two, she had her Ph.D. in sports physiology, with a special interest in the effects of weightlessness on the body's musculature, and she'd been working in the research department of Rice University for the past seven years. On top of that, she had been flying planes since she was twenty-one, and she knew the difference between a yaw and a pitch.

She turned the key in the ignition of her red pickup truck and sat back, ready for the hot ride home, glad she'd worn a T-shirt and her lightweight fatigue pants today. Jennie, like the other astronauts, came to work ready to *work,* and no nonsense about it. She kept her reddish-brown tousled curls short, easy to care for even without a comb and brush. Her slight figure was usually dressed in well-cut but easy-care clothes, and she wore no makeup except when she was on the fried-chicken circuit, doing the PR that was part of every astronaut's job. People had told her that her deep hazel eyes didn't need much enhancing, anyway—they were large and laughing and luminous.

She turned left on Avenue C and started down First Street, wondering once again why the Johnson Space Center didn't rename all their streets. They could have a Moon Walk and a Uranus Drive, not to mention John Glenn, Buzz Aldrin, Neil Armstrong, or Deke Slayton Roads. But the attitude around here was functionalism first, and that went for the architecture of the center as well as the names of the streets. The place was chock-full of white concrete bunkers, much like the junior-high school Jennie remembered so fondly. Oh, it was land-scaped here and there with little goldfish ponds lined with some sparse flower beds, but the basic impression of the center was stark, cold, ready for action.

What a day! she thought as she sped toward the front gates of the center. Nothing but briefings and meetings and then more briefings. But these, too, were considered work for the ninety astronauts currently in the program.

Working for NASA was at least as much PR as it was technical expertise.

She had stopped at an intersection for the guard to cross pedestrians—always an interminable procedure—when she heard a voice directly beside her window.

"Well, Jennie! How's it going?"

She looked down to see Peter Reinhardt, the director of the center, standing on the pavement beside her truck. She always felt a little stuck when she had to talk to Peter. As big boss of the program, supposedly he was the man to know if you wanted to get ahead. But Jennie didn't function that way. She was ambivalent about playing politics, and she remained unconvinced that cozying up to the NASA officials got anybody anywhere.

"Hello, Peter. How are you?"

"Hearing some good things about you, young lady, I can tell you that." He pumped her hand through the open window. "Amazing how far you've come in this short time. Why, I can see great things in your future."

Jennie laughed awkwardly. "Well, I wish I had your crystal ball, then."

"Oh, and Davis just told me about all that weightlessness research you've been doing. I was thinking it would be nice to use that on a flight."

Jennie stopped breathing for a second, then forced herself to start again. Was it possible? Might she really be scheduled for a mission?

"I don't mind telling you that I'd be delighted," she said as calmly as she could. Despite her proud sense of independence and her ambition to clamber to the top, she'd learned long ago which personal traits to hide from the military. Andy had taught her well. "If you want to be one of them, cookie," he'd said when she was first accepted into the astronaut program, "you'll step on your mouth. Anytime you want to say anything that sounds the least bit weird, *don't*."

Peter Reinhardt, an Air Force lieutenant colonel and

a career military man, was now, after three years, only slightly put off by what he considered Jennie's unconventional personality. She certainly couldn't be called a maverick by anyone else's standards, but compared to the stiffs around here, she was positively a wild woman. She simply wasn't a "yes, sir–no, sir" candidate, and she persisted in telling jokes or speaking her mind when everyone else was silent. Even so, Peter grudgingly seemed to like her, treating her almost as a mascot to the troops. At fifty-three, Peter was a product of the old regime, and he still wasn't used to having anyone other than "good old boys" in the program. Air Force men, to Peter, were real men. Everyone else was somehow lacking a crucial gene.

The sound of cars honking behind her shook Jennie from her entranced state of eager anticipation. The crossing guard must have been waving at her for the past five minutes.

"We seem to be holding up traffic," Peter said with a chuckle, "so I'd better let you go. You run along, young lady, and have a very nice evening. I hope to be seeing you again soon." And then he marched off, his military swagger noticeable even though he tried to downplay it these days. Jennie smiled as she watched him go.

She put the truck in gear, then cursed at the traffic jam in front of her. Why? she asked herself as she put the truck into neutral to sit it out. You don't have a hot date or anything, do you? Just be patient. Then she laughed out loud. Patience was definitely not one of the qualities Jennie Jacobs was known for.

The sign on the road that turned left before the airport said DRIVE FRIENDLY, so she tried to, switching on her radio to her favorite country-western station. Dolly Parton sobbed from the speakers, telling her to "Stand By Your Man." Jennie waited for a break in the traffic, then pulled into the fast lane, driving west into the sunset. She'd never wanted anything so much as space flight and had never felt she had so little tolerance for standing around, spinning her wheels.

She'd always had flying on her mind. When she was eight and all her friends were playing with dolls, she was reading every book on flying she could get her hands on and building model planes. As she grew older, she watched every televised launch with a feeling of "It could be me up there." When she was in high school, and her parents, both medical doctors, tried to persuade her that this was just a stage she was going through—and a very long one at that—she went out and got her boyfriend to teach her to hang-glide. Her father was so terrified she was going to kill herself that he agreed to chip in for her flying lessons. And that was it. The minute she was up there, darting through clouds, laughing down at the earth, she was hooked. There was no way she could ever turn back.

And then there was Andy. They'd met during their sophomore year at the University of Wisconsin and hadn't dated anyone else after that. When he went into the U.S. Air Force after they graduated and she started on her Ph.D. at Berkeley, they talked about marriage. Talking led to planning, and it was only a matter of months before they decided they couldn't wait any longer. They were completely unsettled, living in two different states, yet they still wanted that legal bond. The marriage was certainly unconventional: they saw each other on weekends and for brief stretches of time when one of them could get off work. For the two years they were husband and wife, they probably spent all of six months together.

She and Andy moved into their own house when he was finally stationed in Houston, just twelve weeks before he died. It was a small ranch on a nice piece of land just outside Seabrook, on Galveston Bay. Every night now when she pulled into the driveway, she had to look twice to be sure there was no other car parked there, no one in the kitchen preparing the largest avocado salad known to man or woman. It was hard, not living with Andy.

"Well, there you are. I've been wondering when I was going to hear the screech of your brakes." Jennie's neighbor, Susan Jones, stood on her back porch, criticizing Jennie's parking job.

"I do not screech my brakes."

"Do, too. You're the lousiest driver I know. I certainly hope you don't park the missiles like that," Susan clucked, walking over toward her neighbor's yard.

"You don't *park* missiles," Jennie corrected her. "You bring your craft in for a landing and then you taxi down the runway, just like on a plane."

"Yeah, yeah. So I'm a dolt. Just a poor, innocent schoolteacher." Susan, a wide-eyed blonde with long Texas legs, was in her late twenties, married to an engineer, with her first baby on the way. Jennie couldn't have hand-picked better neighbors—being around Susan was like being in the midst of a particularly good party.

"Dolt? How can you say that about my best friend? Well, maybe sometimes." Jennie gave her pal a sly wink. "I love ya anyway, kid."

"Okay, enough with the mush. I'm drowning in it. Tell me, astro-nut, what do you have lined up for tonight?" Susan demanded.

"Oh, I'm pretty well booked. I have about ten plants that are crying to be watered, a carrot cake I've been meaning to bake, my new exercise tape to try out, and— oh, yes, I nearly forgot—I have to darn some socks. Darn!"

Susan made a face. "Scrap it all. I have a better offer."

"Let's hear," Jennie said skeptically. Susan was always trying to drag her out on the town, and she was always balking like a stalled mule.

"Jonesie and I are off to Talbert's for some beers and steaks. I get my pregnant quota of one beer and my steak medium-well, but Jonesie's going for broke. And *you* are coming with us."

"Couldn't possibly." Jennie grinned. "I'm in training."

"Well, you can—" Susan stopped, her mouth ajar. "You didn't! You aren't!" She flung herself across the hedge that separated the two yards. "You're going to fly! You're going up!" She hugged Jennie around the waist and lifted her off the ground.

"Susan, the baby! Put me down. Now wait a second. Just a minute!" Jennie was laughing so hard she couldn't even correct her friend. "I don't know anything for a fact. I just got a hint today—that's all. But the lists won't be posted till Thursday. Are you listening to me? *Nothing* is definite."

"Ooh, a celebration!" Susan's blue eyes were gleaming as though the good news were her own—she was that kind of person. "Wait'll I tell Jonesie!" She was back to her house in a sprint, lunging for the door.

"But, Susan, I can't go with you!" Jennie called. Her words hit the air and fell to earth. She put her head in her hands and rumpled her curls, then shrugged. Well, why *shouldn't* she go? There was nothing wrong with a night out every once in a while, and as a matter of fact, it would be good to be with friends tonight. People who weren't astronauts—wow!

"Oh, all right," she said to convince herself as she walked inside. "Now all I have to figure out is what to wear."

She watered each plant lovingly, picking off a few dead leaves as she went. The place was spotless, the polished wood floors gleaming in the late afternoon sun, but it looked bare and empty to her. It always seemed silly to her to make the place any homier, but she couldn't stop herself. She was a homing-pigeon type. Crocheted and embroidered throw pillows and afghans nestled everywhere, testimony to Jennie's many nights alone at home. She found needlework therapeutic and did it with a frenzy, the way she did everything else, usually keeping three projects going at once. Her home didn't boast much furniture, but it sure had a lot of pillows. Her skinny sixteen-year-old calico cat sat atop one of them, purring loudly up at Jennie.

"Wings, how's my girl?" she asked, giving the animal an impromptu hug. The cat, annoyed at being disturbed, even by Jennie, jumped to the overstuffed velvet armchair and made herself comfortable all over again.

"All right, Miss Grump. Just for that, you can't watch me shower and dress for the great event." Grinning to herself, Jennie carried her attaché case to the master bedroom, whose huge recessed window overlooked a stretch of land leading to the bay. God, how she and Andy used to love gazing out that window! Whenever he was around and felt particularly relaxed, they'd prop themselves on the window seat, their arms tight around each other's waist. Even workaholic Andy, who was never home when he could be up in the sky, would take the time to admire the stark beauty of the landscape— the swooping sea gulls, the multicolored layers of soil and sand and scrub unrolling before him.

She stood there for another moment, her arms clutching the case, and wondered if she'd ever feel whole again. She remembered her marriage to Andy as something close to spectacular. Oh, they'd fought a lot—they were both terrific scrappers—and sometimes when they were both working too hard, things had been strained between them. But all in all, it was pretty super.

Which was why Jennie hated going out, even with Susan and Jonesie. She knew that two years had passed, that it was time to get back in step, that somewhere was probably some other man nearly as wonderful, but still, she hesitated. Work was easy for her, because it was always there—challenging, daring, even dangerous. Now, men were challenging, too, but they were much more elusive. You had to go out and find them.

"What a bummer," Jennie sighed to herself as she tossed her case onto the bed and perused the clothing hanging in her closet. Since she basically wore a uniform to work—and a drab one at that—she loved nothing so much as dressing up. Her wardrobe wasn't extensive, but she'd chosen each piece carefully, with an eye to getting lots of use out of everything. A tussah silk blouse in a delicate jade color and black jeans tucked into her lizard-skin boots—that would do it. Even a little mascara to whoop it up.

By the time she'd showered and dressed, the doorbell was ringing repeatedly. "Coming!" she called, stopping before she got to the front door to put a gold hoop earring in her ear. She turned and waved to Wings, who was peering at her from beneath a throw-rug. "Guard the house, you beast," she told the cat, locking up after herself.

Talbert's was a typical Houston joint, with sawdust on the floor and rough-cut wood tables polyurethaned to a brilliant finish. A good band came on at about nine each night, and sometimes the customers actually got up and moved around to the tunes on the postage-stamp-sized dance floor. The smoky, noisy atmosphere was easy and friendly, and the crowd was generally a nice mix— a few oil barons thrown in with the mechanics for good measure.

Jennie and the Joneses were shown to a choice booth in the back and, after the waitress had taken their drink orders, left to themselves to examine the menu.

"So what's this I hear about your going into space?" Jonesie demanded. "Pretty soon, isn't it?"

Jennie gave Susan a disparaging look. "I really don't think we should jinx it by talking about it, because I don't imagine it's going to happen, but—"

"But you'll talk, because we'll twist your arm," Susan gibed.

Jennie pointedly ignored her friend's delirium. "If I went up now, it would be about a year before I expected to. Usually it takes four years from entry into the program. But with all the flights this year—nearly one a month—NASA has to get their crews somewhere. They're already taking a few veterans back for a second spin, but they'll have to tap the rookies soon. I guess my turn will come."

She sighed hopefully as the waitress brought their beers, and she let her friends toast her possible victory, crossing her fingers under the table that this celebration wasn't premature. One word from Peter Reinhardt did not, by any stretch of the imagination, promise the ultimate goal.

They talked about Susan's work after that—"If I didn't love those damned kids so much, I'd kill 'em, I swear"—and then Jonesie's. Jennie was listening intently to a description of his latest project when a familiar face appeared, making her want to duck under the table.

But he had already seen her. Beer in hand, blond behemoth Dean Bradshaw strode over to her table, followed by a man who was a little taller and looked several years older.

"Well, hello!" Dean stood over Jennie, beaming down. "I didn't think astronauts came to this place."

"I didn't either." There was a strange pause in the proceedings as Jennie and Dean seemed to forget about the people around them. For an instant, Jennie felt as though the two of them were alone in the huge room. She shook her head, remembering her manners. "Dean Bradshaw, these are my next-door neighbors, Susan and Al Jones, the latter better known as Jonesie. And this is one of my fellow companions in the aerospace industry. Dean's an astronaut, too."

"Why, sure!" Jonesie stood up to shake hands, clearly impressed. "I just read that interview you did the other day in the *Journal*. I sure like what you had to say about industry expansion to the heavens, Mr. Bradshaw."

"Thanks." Dean hadn't taken his big blue eyes off Jennie since he'd walked in. "Everybody," he said, finally bringing the other man forward, "this is my brother,

Jim. He's a doctor from New York City, just taking in a conference here."

"Nice to meet you," Jennie said, extending a hand.

"Won't you join us?" Susan asked, starry-eyed to be in the presence of a "real" astronaut as opposed to a next-door-neighbor astronaut.

"Oh, I'm sure Dean and his brother want some time to themselves," Jennie said hastily.

"We've had all the time alone we need." Dean promptly sat beside her. He had to straddle the table leg, which placed their chairs so close he was touching her. When his knee brushed hers, she swallowed hard. On the crowded plane back from Oklahoma the previous day, they'd sat with their own colleagues—pilots with pilots, and mission specialists with mission specialists—so he hadn't had a chance to rib her about her debacle on the parachute apparatus. But since they'd returned, he'd passed her enough times in the hallway for her to know he was still amused by the incident. Why did he make her feel so self-conscious?

"Right. We've caught up on all the family gossip," Jim Bradshaw said, readily accepting one of the empty chairs. "We'd love to join you, if it's no imposition."

Jennie instinctively liked Dean's brother. He had an easy way with people, none of that sense of being out of place among strangers. And she wondered, if she got him alone, what he could tell her about his brother. She was very curious about Dean, although she had vowed never to get curious about any flyer ever again.

"New York, huh?" she said to Jim. "What's it like living there?"

"Well, you have to get used to it, especially when you're an Iowa farm boy like me. But it's exhilarating, and—"

"Like space," Dean cut in.

"I wouldn't know about that," his brother reminded him.

"I wouldn't either—yet."

"But you're going to. I'm placing bets that Dean's next up," Jim told the table at large.

"Hey, why don't you let me blow my own horn?" Dean asked with a laugh.

"Because you know you never will. My friends, this man is the original Mr. Modest."

Sensing a subtle tension between them, Jennie listened to the brothers closely, unable to tell whether they liked each other or just tolerated each other. Probably a little of both, she figured, thinking of herself and her own brother, Chris. She was just about to encourage Jim to reveal more personal insights into Dean when the band started up, playing a slow country number.

"I love that stuff," Jim said. "We don't get enough of it back east."

"It's not bad," Dean agreed. He leaned over the candle that glowed on their table, highlighting his rugged features, and said softly to Jennie, "How about a dance?"

She was acutely aware of Susan, the matchmaker, grinning like a Cheshire cat right next to her. "Well, thanks, but I don't know how."

"Don't be silly." Jim smiled, taking her hand. "Everybody can dance. It's a cinch."

Jennie felt her hand pulled out of Jim's, and her body couldn't help but follow. Dean had practically yanked her out of her seat. "Now just a second," she protested, "I said I didn't want—"

"Well, I'm not the kind of guy who takes no for an answer. I don't even take maybes." Dean's arm warmly encircled her waist, and he led her away from the table and toward the music.

"You're impossible!" she muttered. Then she couldn't say anything else because he was holding her more tightly than he had when he lifted her down from the chute. Her body moved with his, pressing and swaying to the sad melody that sang through the restaurant. She didn't remember the last time she'd danced—or, rather, held on for dear life as a man steered her around the room. She'd always felt like a klutz on a dance floor. But Dean did all the work, making her look more graceful than she felt. She could just relax and let him lead, and suddenly she was dancing—in a manner of speaking.

"I was—" She brought her head up just as he brought his down. They collided with an audible smack.

"Ow!" Dean rubbed his chin, then pulled back to look down into her eyes. "You getting back at me for the other day?"

"Don't be silly. I told you, I'm hopeless at dancing." She was rubbing her head and seeing stars. Then she started laughing. "Now at least we have an excuse to go back to the table." She started to move away from him, but he grabbed her again.

"Are you kidding? I never give up once I latch on to something I want." He had an odd smile on his face, as if he'd just seen her for the first time.

And she was suddenly aware that she'd never *really* looked at him before—not as a man, at any rate. Previously, he'd been the perfect machine, the best flyer around. Over the three years she'd been in the program, they'd been in a few classes together but had hardly had any contact other than that. With eighty-eight other astronauts around, the statistics on the two of them becoming friends had been pretty low. And since losing Andy, Jennie was also twice shy when it came to pilots.

"What do you mean you don't dance?" he whispered as he pulled her closer, murmuring into her hair. "I feel a definite sense of rhythm here. Don't hold back on me, lady."

She was about to answer when she heard the squeals behind her.

"Ooh, isn't that . . . ? It's Dean Bradshaw! I just know it."

"You're right, Tammy. Oh, isn't he just gorgeous!"

Dean didn't let go of Jennie when the two young girls approached and asked for his autograph. He just smiled politely and said he didn't usually give them. Jennie felt very much like the odd man out, even with his warm arms wrapped around her, as the two teeny-boppers circled them like hungry sharks. One was staggering on what had to be her first pair of high heels, and her makeup was smeared. The other, less garish, was dressed in a tight, short skirt and an I LOVE HOUSTON sweat shirt.

"My friend here is an astronaut, too." Dean smiled at Jennie. "This is Dr. Jennifer Jacobs. Maybe she'll oblige you."

The one with the teetering stance frowned, then shrugged.

"Nice to meetcha," muttered the other girl, quickly shifting her attention back to Dean. Even when the number ended and the two of them wandered back to the table, the girls followed. For the next twenty minutes, it was impossible to get rid of the two groupies.

"My turn," Jim said to Jennie, pushing back his chair. "You two looked so good out there, I have to try and top it."

"No, honest. My feet are coming off," Jennie demurred.

Dean glanced sharply at his brother. "I've really had a day, pal," he confessed. "What do you say we shove off?"

"Sure I can't persuade you?" Jim smiled down at Jennie with such warmth, she almost gave in. "Just half a dance? A quarter?" he cajoled when she shook her head.

"I'm sure." She grinned, then looked at Dean, who seemed rather watchful, as if he were waiting for something to happen. He didn't really seem to want to break up the party, but he did look a little beat. Well, at least he's human! Jennie thought with relief. Mr. Perfect Astronaut has to rest sometimes, too.

"In that case, I relinquish my turn till next time. It's been a real pleasure." Jim got up, taking Jennie's hand again. "Hope to see you again before I leave."

"Yes, me too." She smiled at his gallantry. He seemed like a bona fide party person, the kind of guy who could dance till dawn and still be ready for a hard day at work.

"I'll see you at the Center tomorrow," Dean told her quietly as he began moving away from the table. His attitude intrigued her. There they'd been, blissfully locked in each other's arms, and now he was perfectly cool.

As the two men left, the groupies trailing behind them, Susan laughed out loud and nodded in the direction of the door. "I think he'll have to use an acetylene torch to get those two off his back. Not that I really blame them— gorgeous hunk like that," she said mischievously with a glance at her husband. "He certainly caused a sensation." She looked curiously at Jennie, who was lost in thought. "Do male astronauts always have that effect on women?"

Jennie laughed. "My dear, they have the pick of the crop. Whereas, for the women, it's an entirely different story. We're still sort of freaks—people shy away from us. And you can imagine that any man who got close enough might want to tell a few of his buddies about the conquest. We can't risk our reputations like that. Not with good old NASA breathing down our necks and judging how 'appropriate' our behavior is. No, for us lady flyers, it's a lonely life."

"Well, that doctor fella seemed interested enough," Jonesie said, reaching for his wallet.

"You think so?" Jennie smiled absently, quickly stuffing a twenty-dollar bill into Jonesie's hand. She wouldn't let him give it back.

As they drove home, Jennie sitting quietly in the back seat of their sedan, she thought about her own statement again. Was she really a freak, destined to sit out the coming dances of life until it was her turn to fly? Why had she felt so free this evening, floating in a man's arms again? Was it because he wasn't just any man, but another astronaut, who wouldn't consider her a freak? Or was she simply ripe to be swept off her feet? And by Dean Bradshaw, of all people. She didn't trust herself, so she decided to banish the fanciful thoughts from her mind.

"Want a nightcap, Jen?" Susan asked as they arrived home.

"No, thanks. Got to get my health sleep. You two are super—thanks for a wonderful evening." She hugged them both, and to her surprise, she felt happy and warm as they left her at her door.

- 2 -

It was a cool morning at the space center. According to the weatherman on Jennie's truck radio, the August heat wave had broken, and everyone was in for relief. She could see as she walked down the nearly deserted NASA paths that the coolness had signaled some of the guys to step up their physical conditioning—before it was too late and the assignments were already handed out.

"Hey, guys, how ya doin'?" Jennie called to two of the astronauts who'd entered the program at the same time she had. They were huffing along near Building 9A, trying to make four miles before hopping into the simulator for their daily training.

NASA didn't have any physical fitness program per se; you were just supposed to keep in shape so you wouldn't get sick and be bumped from your flight. But there were easier ways than running yourself into a hot frenzy, thought Jennie, who was a racquetball nut herself. At least the courts were air-conditioned and the game had some challenge to it.

She swung open the gray metal door of 9A and hurried

up the black iron staircase to the cruise-station simulator. Ann Lorge, her trainer, was already at the computer network down below, and she waved to Jennie absently, keeping her eye on the green screens in front of her.

"What's the stock market doing today?" Jennie joked.

"Lordie, you think I know? With what they pay me here, I couldn't invest in galactic dust!" Ann looked up at last, her cherubic face slightly weary and haggard. "Hi, sweetheart. How was Oklahoma? No, don't tell me. You were voted the parachutist least likely to succeed."

"You got it!"

Ann was a wonder woman, no doubt about it. At forty, she had been with NASA longer than she liked to remember. She'd started as a secretary, and then, when promotion policies became slightly easier for women, she'd marched directly to the top of the ladder. Jennie wondered sometimes whether Ann really longed to fly, just as she did, but she'd never had the guts to ask her.

Andy used to tell her she projected too much, that she assumed everyone wanted what she wanted, liked what she liked, and loathed what she loathed with exactly the same intensity. But she really didn't think he was right about that. It was hard for Jennie to look at people and not imagine what they were going through.

She knew that "sensitivity" was something a woman was expected to have as a birthright, but she seemed to have an overabundance of it.

Her impressionability didn't help in her dealings with the military higher-ups or the NASA personnel. She knew they saw her as a fragile flower, someone to handle with kid gloves, and that worked against her. Then there was her damned inferiority complex. She was always certain things were her fault even when they weren't. Never about her own research—she was a solid scientist and knew it—but this astronaut business really had her flummoxed a lot of the time. She just didn't do things the way the other candidates did. Whenever Jennie Jacobs messed up, she did it in a splashy way. When she got reprimanded for it, she tried hard not to take the criticism personally, but she usually failed in the attempt. Even Ann's gentle gibing hurt a little.

"If they ever make me get on that thing again..." Jennie let the words trail off. Of course they would. Until the day you sat strapped into your seat and heard the familiar countdown to liftoff, you'd be pushing and pulling your body and your mind to the limit. "Well, what are we waiting for?" Jennie grinned down at her. "Can I have the trajectory and payload of the day?"

"Stay right there. It'll be coming out of my machine in a sec. And as soon as Bradshaw deigns to arrive, we'll get started."

Jennie's cheerful expression froze. "But... you don't mean I'm stuck with *him* for four hours? We've never assigned together." I can't do it, she thought in a panic. I'll freeze trying to think straight if he's staring at me with those baby blues of his.

"Hey, don't complain. He knows more than all the rest of us put together. Not to mention the fact that he's gorgeous," Ann added slyly.

"Oh, but he's so good at what he does—I'm going to feel so inferior. Bad for my psyche, Ann," she grumbled, knowing his expertise wasn't the only source of her discomfiture. Swinging open the metal door of the similulator, she added, "Anything I can do, he can do better. And he'll let me know it, too."

"But that's what those pilot types are taught to do, Jen. Hell, if you spent the better part of your life racing through the atmosphere upside down in a flimsy T-38 and came back to tell about it, you'd think you were perfect, too." She chuckled, then suddenly realized what she'd said. "Oh, my God, Jennie, I...I didn't mean that. I'm such a dodo. I just wasn't thinking."

"Forget it. Listen, Ann, I know you're not capable of being cruel." She went inside the cruise station and sat heavily on one of the plastic molded seats, suddenly set back a few years. She hated feeling vulnerable—hated it. After all this time, why hadn't she healed, for heaven's sake?

Andy had been a pilot, too, one of the finest and bravest. He thought being an astronaut was okay for the other guys—including his wife—but for him, it was the daring adventure of a tiny jet plane that made life worth living. Well, they all flew T-38's, and they all joked about how much jiggling, shaking, and buffeting one body could take in that tin can. The thing about a jet was that if the engines quit, you'd fall like a rock out of the sky. Unlike parachute or centrifuge maneuvers, there was no do-over, no second chance with a dead T-38. Andy had spun crazily all the way down, they'd told her. That was over two years ago, and she could still feel the terrible loneliness every time she walked into their house.

"Is this seat taken?" asked a quiet voice to her right. "I thought I'd join you for a while, if that's okay with you."

"Be my guest," she told Dean as calmly as she could, shoving aside memories with a quick shake of her head. "Ann's bringing up the info right away."

"Last night was fun. We should do it again." He looked so rakish, so much the space adventurer, she had to catch her breath. Nobody could wear a jumpsuit like Bradshaw. For other men around here, clothing was just something functional to cover the skin. With Dean, it was an enhancement. The fabric molded itself to those broad shoulders and firmly muscular thighs, somehow throwing them into higher relief.

It was true, he was an exceptional-looking man. His angular features blended in just the right way, and his body was massive but graceful. As he closed the door behind them both, shutting out the world, she began to feel slightly light-headed. She'd never really had a serious conversation with him, so she had no idea whether the interior of the man matched the surface, but after last night, she had a certain desire to look deeper. That was scary. She'd always assumed she didn't really want to know another pilot.

"Sure. And I liked your brother." She swiveled in her chair as the door opened again and Ann handed her the printouts. "Oh, thanks, Ann." A quick scan told her they'd be taking quite a trip today.

The motion-based cruise-station simulator was about as close as you could get to the real thing. The huge gray box could rotate within six degrees of freedom from horizontal landing to vertical launch position. An astronaut working inside would feel the yaw, pitch, and roll motions of the actual craft and would hear the noise of the engines and the wind around him. He'd also feel the bump of landing. The only thing the machine couldn't do was imitate the anti-gravity state. That was the wild card.

"Let me see that a minute." Dean took the plans from her and hastily scanned the first three pages. "What sadist made this up?"

"I did," Ann laughed. "I'm cracking the whip today, you two. Have a good flight." She swung the metal door shut behind her, leaving Jennie and Dean to assemble their material and get into position for the mock launch.

Ann's voice crackled through the loudspeaker. "We're going for liftoff. You two strapped in?"

"Ready and counting," Dean asserted.

Their computers began flashing, showing them the position of the craft. And then, as Ann began the countdown, they could feel the simulator working. Jennie pressed the small of her back against the hard seat and watched the numbers on her dial. It was her job as mission specialist to monitor what every machine was doing. All Dean had to worry about, the lucky stiff, was being flight commander.

Dean switched a few toggles to the right, and Jennie watched closely to make sure she knew what he was doing. As she reached her hand over to pull a switch, it brushed his. Startled by the contact, she drew her fingers away rapidly.

"What's wrong?" he murmured.

"Nothing." But she knew he could see she was lying.

Ann had them on automatic now, but they could never be too careful about things like that. When she sent them higher, through a difficult series of technical obstacles, they both had to think hard. Problem-solving in space, improvising when you thought everything looked so clear-cut but wasn't, was something every astronaut had to learn.

About an hour into the lesson, Ann asked them to assume that they'd lost contact with their tracking station.

Dean turned to Jennie with a smile. "What would you do?"

"Just keep at it. They'll find us again." There were twelve tracking stations around he world, from the U.S. to Spain to Australia. Every time they were in range, you could communicate with one of the stations on earth. Once out of range, you were in a silent phase.

"Maybe they won't. Maybe we'll be lost in space for days, even months. Could you hack it?"

She made a face at him. "Highly unlikely that would happen, Commander Bradshaw." What would that be like? she wondered, the fantasy flitting across her brain. She'd never been alone with Dean until now, and already she felt as if the air were too thin. He wiped all the professional stamina out of her with those dynamite eyes of his.

"Oh, you doubt me. Well, lady, you never know up there. However, if the company proved compatible, we might just make it."

How could he make the simple word *compatible* sound sexy? She looked at him, feeling the pulse in her temples start to pound. The effect he had on her was very peculiar, and she tried thinking about anything that would take her mind off him. But it proved impossible. He, on the other hand, seemed totally unruffled.

"Incredible, isn't it?" Dean murmured as he sat back and looked at the panels in front of him. Ever-changing photos of the earth flashed before them as their vehicle rolled and turned on its axis. "We orbit this planet once every ninety minutes. I mean, that's how long it takes to put a new starter in my car."

Jennie laughed and completed her guidance system directions on the computer. "And we get sixteen sunrises and sunsets a day up here."

"Really? I never knew that." Dean looked astonished.

"Hey, I can't believe I knew something you didn't," she said, secretly amazed and pleased with herself.

He looked at her seriously for a minute. "You know a lot, lady. Word gets around," he explained when she looked at him quizzically.

He was really bolstering her morale, and it was just what she needed. She grinned, rubbing her hands together in anticipation. "Lord, I can't wait to get up there! Not that I expect to be picked this time, of course. I understand they're posting the new assignments Thursday."

"Right. For the big one—the mission they've kept secret for so long. I have a hunch . . ." He let his sentence trail off, but the look on his face was unmistakable.

"Oh? I suppose you think you've got it," Jennie said coolly. She was jealous, no doubt about it. Although he hadn't actually gone up, Dean had already served as Capcom for one flight, which was close to being a standby for a lead actor in a theatrical production. The Capcom trained with the flight crew and therefore knew the payload and the particular problems of the specific craft backward and forward. It was true; Dean was more ready than she to go up.

"You never know you've got it till they put your name up in lights." He leaned away from the control board and looked at her intently. "You like to fly, huh? I've heard you're a mean eagle up there."

"Haven't gotten much practice lately," Jennie confessed. "But I love it, sure."

"Well, you'll have to take me up sometime. Show me your stuff."

She bit her lip, anxious again, and for no reason. Yes, she was a good flyer, but compared to him, she was a rank amateur in an airplane. There would be nothing at all she could "show" him that he hadn't mastered years ago. "I'm afraid I'd disappoint you, cowboy. I'm not that good."

"Bet you are. I like flying with someone. I can get to know them that way. Know them well."

"Uh-huh." She, too, knew that flying with someone else was a very personal matter. It created a bond between pilot and co-pilot, something they shared that the rest of the world didn't participate in. When they were up there, no one else and nothing else mattered. The world could vanish, and they would be riding high together, laughing at the void.

Since Andy's death two years ago, she'd sold their planes, taking much less than she should have for them because she was so eager to have the whole thing over with. She still flew, of course, but it wasn't the same.

"You going to follow these docking plans, lady? Or is it my move?" Dean asked when her hands sat idle on the controls. They'd been working for nearly three hours now, and she was feeling the fatigue.

"Sorry, cowboy. I'll get us back."

"How come you keep calling me 'cowboy'?"

At that point, Ann interrupted them and began to talk them through the various preparations for re-entry. Jennie tried to force her mind back to the work, but she was terribly distracted for some reason. Dean's seemingly innocuous question about flying together had set her off, and that upset her. She hated it when anything got in the way of her work.

The simulator let them down gently, returning to its original position with a decided thump. As she and Dean made their way out of the cabin for their evaluation, his hand lightly brushed the small of her back, and a funny shudder went though her. Had he really touched her, or was she imagining it?

"Excellent work, guys," Ann commented as they came down the stairs toward her. "You two have a nice partnership up there—wouldn't be a bad idea to pair you on a flight."

"I wouldn't mind it," Dean said, poker-faced.

"Whatever you say, Ann." Jennie suddenly felt a trigger go off inside her. First Peter, now Ann seemed to be suggesting that she be assigned. The crews were set long in advance, and everyone around the center assumed that Dean's name was going to be first up this time. But if Jennie had been posted for next year, could they still bump her forward in the schedule? She positively itched to go into space.

What would it be like to go up with Dean Bradshaw? He got her so rattled on earth, she'd probably fall apart without any bearings to latch on to. His effect on her was as potent as anti-gravity was supposed to be.

"Well," Ann continued, turning back to her green screens, "we'll just have to see." And with that, she told them to go get some lunch and have a nice afternoon. Jennie was ready to burst. Here they were, discussing the most crucial issue of life, and her trainer was telling her to go get a sandwich!

Somehow, the day came to an end. The nice thing about it was that it was a pure eight hours of hard work, no briefings, no classes, no PR. So when Jennie got back in her truck at five-thirty, she felt nicely used, rubbed to a fine sheen by the assignments she'd tackled and completed.

She was busy hoping and wishing for that major assignment when she spotted a lone figure hitchhiking by the main gate. As she drove closer, she realized, to her total amazement, that it was Dean Bradshaw. Now, that was peculiar. She'd heard the man was practically attached to his red Corvette Stingray by an umbilical cord.

Cars passed right by him, she noted as she inched forward in the line. No, that wasn't exactly true. Several drivers stopped to say something to the brawny blond astronaut, but no one picked him up. Probably weren't going his way.

She rolled down her window, saying, "I take it you need a lift."

"You got it, lady. Someone rammed right into my car while I was up there with you, simulating a daring mission. It just got towed."

He sounded so forlorn, she couldn't laugh. "Where're you going?"

"Shoreacres. You wouldn't by any chance be heading for that general vicinity?"

Shoreacres was the town just before Jennie's, right on Galveston Bay. Strange that she had worked in the same program with this man for three years now and never knew he was practically a neighbor.

"I happen to be going close. Hop in—I'll drop you off." She felt odd sitting next to him in her truck, her private province. It was odder still to notice how her palms suddenly froze up on the steering wheel. What was she getting all upset about? she asked herself as she pulled out onto the main road and started for home. He'd seen her drive before—at least in a spacecraft simulator. And yet, along the way, she couldn't get over the feeling that he was watching her every move, every flick of her eyelashes. It annoyed and tickled her at the same time.

"So, how do you think we did up there today?" He leaned his head back on the seat, closing his magnetic blue eyes.

She glanced over at the relaxed form beside her and smiled. "Well," she ventured, "*I* did beautifully."

"You want to fight about who's better?" He put his dukes up in mock battle position. "I'm a great wrestler," he added suggestively.

She laughed it off, but she suddenly got an image of

the two of them rolling around on her Oriental rug. The picture in her mind made her hand jerk the steering wheel to the right. He glanced at her with a little half smile on his dazzling face. He was pleased that he'd gotten to her, dammit!

"Sorry, but I always take up a couple of lanes at once if I can," she joked. Jennie, straighten up and fly right! she ordered herself.

They had just reached the outskirts of Shoreacres, a pretty suburb with neat rows of town houses done in white and beige stucco. "Hey," he said, "you never answered my question."

"Which one?"

"Why you call me 'cowboy.'"

She laughed and looked directly ahead at the road. "Oh, you know how you get impressions of people just by the way they come across? I can't help but see you in a Stetson and chaps, riding herd on a bunch of steers. It's just the way you look to me." The truth was that she went for the Marlboro-man image hook, line, and sinker. Dean's tough build, his sensual walk, and the casual but determined placement of his body made her think of a wild bronco sensing his turf. Lately she couldn't take her eyes off him when he was in motion.

"A horse threw me once. That was the closest I came to cowboydom." He was wearing a lopsided grin. He suddenly slung his arm over the back of her seat, and she felt an urgent need to push down harder on the accelerator. "Want to know my first impression of you?"

"Sure." He probably thought she was some metal-headed scientist, more at home in a white lab coat than in a flame-retardant space suit.

"Turn here, Tuscaloosa Road. I thought you were like a hummingbird, too fast to catch. Was I right?"

She couldn't look at him. The air in the cab was growing closer; it was getting harder to breathe. She shook her head in a noncommittal way, but clearly it was no answer for him. He leaned over and touched her hand, which was suddenly trembling as though she'd dipped it in ice water.

"Jennifer Jacobs, I've got something to show you. Why don't you come in for a second? Here, park around the side."

The house he indicated sat all by itself, like a cactus in the middle of a desert. It was very modern, with oddly shaped windows and a spiral stairway she could see through the glass panel that extended up the center of the house. Jennie parked and just sat there, trying to catch her breath.

"I don't bite," he said in a low, rumbling voice. He just sat there, too.

"Well, I do have plans for tonight," she lied, fighting the feeling of being overwhelmed by him.

"I won't keep you." His tone was insistent, and when she looked over at him, she noticed the determined gleam that penetrated down to the depths of his ocean-blue eyes. It was like looking into the center of a wave that was just about to swamp you. You had to swim into it or get knocked down.

"Okay. Just for a minute," she agreed awkwardly.

He led her around the back of the house, where a small tropical garden bloomed in the arid, sandy soil. Just as she could see the bay from her bedroom window, you could see it from here. A different view but with the same feeling.

"How about a beer?" he asked, opening the back door for her.

"I'll take a cup of tea," she said, feeling like a schoolgirl. "Your brother, Jim—"

"Went home today," he said abruptly. "It's just the two of us. Tea coming up." He walked in front of her into the small galley kitchen and set a kettle to boil. Then he took out several containers of exotic tea leaves and asked her to choose.

She laughed and threw up her hands. "I only know from Lipton's," she confessed. "You pick." Then her eye spotted a neat pile of laundry, ready to be taken out. The item on top was too irresistible to let pass. "What in the world!"

"Aren't they great?" Dean grinned, his huge hands covering hers for a moment as he took the item from her. "Guys at flight training school had these made for me the day I got my astronaut status."

"Not only have I never seen black satin sheets with red airplanes embroidered on them," she said, chuckling, "I've never even imagined them." But her mind was saying something entirely different: *When did you use these, and who was she?*

"Those flyers were a pretty creative bunch," he acknowledged. The kettle began to sing, and he turned off the heat under it. "I love flying!" he said in a sudden burst of spontaneity. "There are few things in life I feel so strongly about, Jen. Except—here! Come here! This is what I wanted to show you."

She walked over to him, and he unselfconsciously moved her in front of him before the large bay window. He pointed over her right shoulder and left his arm lying there, which caused her to swallow hard. "Will they be anywhere near that good, do you think? Those sixteen sunrises and sunsets?"

The sun out beyond them was a red ball of flame in the west, highlighting the dusky sky with flamboyant streaks of crimson and orange. It looked like an explosion somewhere off in the distance.

"I hope so," she murmured, wondering at this supposedly tough guy's sensitivity in wanting to share the beauty of a sunset. The arm on her shoulder was like a siren's song, tantalizing her with its weight and its closeness. She had the strangest sensation, as if she were being wrapped in velvet.

"I hope we get to see them together." Then he slowly turned her around, his free hand steering her waist lightly, so delicately. The other arm curled over her back, drawing her closer. "Did I ever tell you how much I'd like to get to know you?" he asked.

But she couldn't answer because he was kissing her now, a hard, firm pressure on her lips that made thinking impossible. She was intoxicated by him, lulled by his power and his insistent physical presence. The man had crawled inside her very soul and commanded her to pay attention.

How long had it been since she'd kissed anyone, let alone a man as compelling as Dean Bradshaw? It was almost as if she had forgotten the simple activity of man and woman, clinging, enjoying, tasting the fruits of one another's delighted interest. She didn't know if she even liked Dean Bradshaw, but she did know she couldn't stop kissing him.

Their lips parted, then returned to home base, opening to receive the other's eager caress. Jennie didn't know what to do with her hands, so she did nothing, letting him lead, letting him give her everything he could offer. He acted as determined with her as he was in his work; but even as he took what he wanted from her, he seemed to be asking permission. He was not all steel; there was an element of shyness there, too.

They drew apart breathlessly, and she felt a sudden loss. She was also blushing as she hadn't in years, and it made her mad that something as insignificant as a kiss should set her off this way.

"Well..." Dean said quietly, those midnight eyes never leaving hers.

"Yes, well." She had no idea what to say, so she said the next thing that came into her head. "How come this took you three years?" she asked, hoping she didn't sound too eager.

He smiled, not looking at all embarrassed. "I don't know. Maybe I needed the time to work up some momentum? No, that's not it." He drew her closer. "I can't really tell you. But once I get going, lady..." He let the declaration trail off.

They stood there for a minute, transfixed, and Jennie

suddenly had a moment's doubt. What was she doing here with this man she scarcely knew? After all this time, it was too much, too soon. "I really have to be going," she said, knowing she couldn't possibly stick around any longer without becoming utterly giddy.

"Don't you want that tea?"

"Uh, no, thanks."

"You always stop when you're ahead, huh?"

"That's it. Guess I'll see you in the morning."

"Sure."

She was at the door when she thought to ask, "Do you want a ride tomorrow? It's on my way."

"Uh-uh. Nothing's wrong with my car." He pointed around the side of the house, and she noticed a shiny red fender sticking out in plain view. "Hank gave me a ride this morning so we could discuss a new flight plan for the tester next week. I was just standing there hitching, waiting for you." He gave her a devilish grin.

She was more dumbfounded than annoyed that he'd lied to her. After three whole years, it was becoming very clear that he was more than professionally interested in her. It was also clear, despite the fact that they were in competition for the most important work of their lives, that she felt the same about him.

"Oh, really? Dean, listen, this is—"

"This is nice," he pronounced, seeing her briskly to the door. "It's *very* nice. And if you deny it, I may try something more drastic next time."

Her knees were shaking as she drove home, clacking together so badly that it was hard to keep her usual control of the truck. She didn't know if she was hot or cold, happy or sad, smart or dumb. All she knew was that there was no gravity whatsoever in her very light head, and that she would not sleep a wink that night.

- 3 -

FOR ABOUT AN hour after Jennie left, Dean tried to read *Space News Roundup*, finding it difficult to concentrate on anything at all, let alone the orbital maneuvering vehicle that might extend the reach of space transport to twenty-three thousand miles above the earth.

Well, he'd finally taken the plunge. Actually, he hadn't intended anything of the sort, but something had come over him when Jennie was that close. Hell, he didn't even know the woman—didn't know what she ate for breakfast or what her father did for a living or if she'd ever been married. For years he'd seen her around the center and had tried to fight the feeling that swarmed through him like a busy hive of bees every time he looked at her. What he felt about her *was* just an impression, after all. When you didn't know somebody, you could make up all sorts of things.

But there was this dream he'd had. Sounded stupid— too dumb to tell her about—but the dream had stayed with him for weeks. He was outside the craft, floating in space, trying to fix something that had come loose. Suddenly, his lifeline had snapped, and he was moving off, away from the fixed orbit. He started to panic. But then a hand reached out to him, and he grabbed it. It was a small but strong hand, hardly big enough for his large one to hang on to. He let its slight pressure move him back effortlessly, and then he was caressing her face, looking into her glistening hazel eyes.

The strange thing was, he'd seen this woman around for years and had never done anything about it. But that was like him, he supposed—letting the easy stuff come to him and neglecting the hard stuff. He wasn't always too swift with women—could never seem to think of the right thing to say at the right time. But as the dream stayed with him, he decided to risk it, to try to get to know her. What the hell—maybe it meant nothing, but then again, maybe it would mean everything in time.

He thought about that night at Talbert's. The closeness of her tight, small body, the overwhelming excitement he'd felt when he was dancing with her, as if the world might explode around them and there they'd be—two beings clinging together. Too bad he'd been with his brother that night.

He ought to call Jim, he thought, getting up to make himself a cup of tea. Patch things up, make up for that dumb argument they'd had. Seemed every time they got together they ended up arguing about some little thing. Despite their affection, there was always an underlying tension between them.

But Dean didn't want to call Jim. All he wanted to do was sit around and think about Jennie Jacobs—the way her husky voice matched her dark red-brown curls, the way her lips had soothed his as they touched softly and intimately.

He waited for the kettle to boil and poured water over his tea bag, watching the color turn from clear to dark amber. Her image swam up at him from the cup, and he stared at it for a while without sipping.

"Damn!" he muttered, walking over to the leather couch and taking the phone in his lap. "I'm acting like a kid who's just had his first date."

He dialed the New York number and waited five rings. As he was about to hang up, he heard the receiver being picked up at the opposite end. "Hello! Jim, is that you?"

"Dean, I didn't expect to hear from you so soon," boomed Jim's cheery voice.

"Just wanted to make sure you got back all right. Those commercial pilots don't know what the heck to do with a 747."

"Well, I'm safe and sound. What's on your mind?" Jim sounded rushed, as if he'd had a hard day that wasn't over yet.

"Listen, about that blowout you and I had—" Dean began.

'Hey, I can't blame you for getting mad. I come down to your territory and start mouthing off about all my successes, all those conquests—I must have sounded like a Class-A turkey."

"Yeah, as a matter of fact, you did," Dean said softly.

"But hell," Jim continued cheerfully, "can I help it if ladies throw themselves in my path?"

"It's true," Dean answered good-naturedly. "You're the original man who charms the pants off anything in skirts. Know what, Jim? I think it might be good for you to find one—just one—and concentrate on her."

"Don't I wish I had the time to get something going!" Jim sighed. "And speaking of lovely ladies, how about that astronaut? Jennie, wasn't it?"

"What about her?" Dean was instantly on guard. He didn't like his brother mentioning her.

"Nice lady, that's all. What are you barking at me for?"

Dean cleared his throat, wondering at the intensity of his own reaction. "Jim, don't you think both of us would be a lot happier if we weren't so competitive?"

"Who's competitive? Not me, brother. Look, take care of yourself, will you? And give me a call when you get the assignment."

"Thanks for rooting for me. Good night, Jim."

There was a click at the other end, then silence. Dean laid the receiver over his knee and imagined his brother, laughing, happy, flirting with countless women. He loved his brother, but he didn't understand a lot of things about him.

The uncradled phone began making an unpleasant buzzing sound, which snapped Dean from his reverie. He hung up, then took a deep swallow of the tea. It was cold. He picked up the manual for the T-89 he was supposed to take out the following week, and, kicking off his shoes, he wandered to the kitchen. There was some cold chicken sitting uncovered in the refrigerator, and a hunk of unidentifiable cheese. That'd do for dinner.

He ate; he read the manual; he thought about Jennie, then about Jim. Then he reminded himself that if there was one thing a flyer absolutely had to have, it was tunnel mentality, similar to tunnel vision. You had to think straight about your craft and nothing else when you were flying; you simply couldn't afford to let your mind wander. Particularly with the new T-89's.

The jet was like the T-38 but trickier, with a roll control so sensitive you could invert the thing with a flick of the wrist. Only trouble with these babies was that once you started the T-89 rolling, it could be hard to control— so hard, in fact, that it would occasionally defy any effort to right it and soar right down to earth, taking the pilot along for his last ride.

His work was certainly rigorous—and dangerous. Why did he get such a kick out of it? Maybe because it took his mind off the mundane, which was of no interest to him. Since he was a kid growing up on his father's farm, he'd known the value and the satisfaction of hard work and self-discipline. He'd always been shy, too quiet for his own good, ready to busy himself in chores or school-work rather than have a conversation with a stranger. The deceptive part was the hard core of steel behind his reticence. People expected one thing from him and often got another. He didn't mind turning the tables that way, because he never wanted anyone to take him for granted. He'd been told that his striking good looks, his muscular body, and his will of steel added up to one dynamite combination, but he'd never bragged about himself. Apparently, what he was spoke for itself.

Jim, on the other hand, bragged all the time—exactly why, Dean had never figured out. His brother always seemed to have so much going for him. Their mother used to wash his mouth out with soap when he got particularly boastful, but that didn't stop him. Jim was brash, successful in almost everything he tried, a natural crowd pleaser. Considered less handsome than Dean, he still managed to date more, to get around more. He was proud of his ability to charm people—particularly women.

Dean, however, was a loner. At a very early age he knew he wanted the military—and he was intuitive enough to know he'd wanted it partly because it was something his brother wasn't the least bit interested in. He was certainly no war monger, just conservative, preferring a weekend of solitary fishing to a booze-filled night on the town with the guys. As for girls, well, he generally let them come to him—which they did with alacrity. There was Laurie in high school, and the next summer there was Alison. In college, where he signed up for ROTC, there was a string of girls, but he never got very serious about any of them. And then came flight training school, when his steady was an airplane. He was too wound up in learning everything he could about flying to consider women—or, rather, one special woman. Consequently, he didn't meet Marilyn until he was twenty-five. He would have married her, too, if it hadn't been for Jim . . .

Now, ten years later, he just didn't know whether marriage was even right for him. He was so set in his ways, so loony about his career. What woman could stand for that? Only another astronaut, probably. Another astronaut? He shook his head, then buried himself in the manual. No time to be thinking about romance. He had work to do.

* * *

Jennie didn't think she could get through the next day, but somehow the hours passed and it was suddenly Thursday, time for the lists to be posted outside the public relations office in Building 2.

"Kind of like waiting for your college board scores, isn't it?" murmured Darlene McFadden, one of the other female astronauts on Jennie's level. She was a crack engineer, terribly smart, and large and strong enough to do maneuvers outside the spacecraft. Most of the women were too small even to be fitted with pressurized space suits because of the prohibitive price. Jennie looked at Darlene's tall, solid form with envy, thinking her size probably gave her a considerable edge.

"You're not kidding. Either that, or like after a play audition, when they're about to post who got what part."

"Well, good morning!" Dean Bradshaw looked positively radiant, as if he knew he was in for a good day.

"Oh, you. Get lost, will ya?" Darlene gave him one of her playful shoves, the kind that could knock a man to the ground. Dean didn't budge. "If there's one thing I can't stand," she said, "it's the straight-A student worrying about whether he passed the test."

Jennie looked at him closely from under her dark fringe of eyelashes. Things would undoubtedly be just the same between them—they were both professionals, after all—and yet she couldn't help but wonder what he was thinking. Her own mind was completely split in two, and every once in a while, thoughts of Dean crowded out thoughts of getting the assignment.

A small crowd of anxious-looking men and a few women had gathered behind them. Everyone was going to be late to work today, but NASA tolerated that up to a point when announcements were being posted.

"C'mon, Dan!" yelled Jeff Davis, a senior flyer. "Let's have those lists before we tear the place apart."

"All right, keep your shirt on," the harried PR director

told him through the plate-glass panel of his neat little
cubicle. "Flight selection just sent down the memo—
I'm trying to get it in order."

"Who wants order? We want info!" called Darlene.

Dan Abrams, a cherubic round man in his early fifties,
sporting a goatee and thick mustache, staggered out of
his office bearing the precious announcement. At least
twenty eager astronauts followed him down the hall to
the bulletin board, where he posted the latest NASA
News.

The memo read:

For Immediate Release:

NASA ANNOUNCES
UPDATED FLIGHT CREW ASSIGNMENTS

The National Aeronautics and Space Administration today announced the assignment of the next
Space Shuttle flight crew and the rescheduling of
some other crews for upcoming missions.

STS 81-D
Late August launch

OV203: OAST ops/ComSat deploys
Possible secondary launch objective

Jeff Davis, Commander
Dean Bradshaw, Pilot
Darlene McFadden, Mission Specialist
Rob Callahan, Mission Specialist
[3rd MS, to be announced]
James Donadio, Payload Specialist

Jennie read the names over twice, then turned away
from the board, hoping the pain didn't show on her face.

They'd already picked a woman for the flight, which left her out, even though there was still one mission specialist to be chosen. She tried to tell herself that it didn't matter, that there was plenty of time for her, but she didn't bother to read any farther down the list for the future missions mentioned. The truth of the matter was, she had wanted this one. Getting one a year from now seemed like such a comedown.

"I'd invite you out to celebrate, but you're probably not in the mood," said a voice close to her left shoulder.

"What? Oh, hey, congratulations. I mean, everyone knew you'd make it, but still, it's nice to be legal." She looked at Dean and saw the disappointment in her face mirrored in his warm blue eyes.

"I'm getting fitted for my suit this afternoon—want to come watch?" he asked suggestively. "I hear I'm gonna be a knockout."

"No," she said flatly. "I don't want to *watch* you do anything. Do you understand?" She looked at him intently, not caring that her competitive edge was showing. Besides, she was always outspoken, and if he was the least bit interested in getting to know her, it was better they begin on honest territory.

"Jennie—" he began, but she was already on her way out the door, off to Ann's office for some stats on the PAM cargo she was supposed to fly. The kicker was, she'd be flying it in a gray metal box on earth. She was beginning to think her whole life was a simulation.

She whisked down the hall and out into the humid morning, marching straight to Building 7, trying to block out the despairing thoughts that filled her brain to overflowing. Dammit, she deserved the assignment. She'd worked so hard, progressed so far. Her research was coming along beautifully, and she desperately wanted a chance to try it out. But what could a grounded physiologist do, for heaven's sake?

"You ready for me?" she asked as she stuck her head

into Ann's office. The place was a mess, as usual, with the in-box flowing over into the out-box, and the posters on the wall hanging at lopsided angles. Ann had a terrific collection of moon rocks, gathered by Neil Armstrong himself, but they seemed strategically placed so that any- one who wasn't watching would trip over them.

"What? Oh, come in, Jennie. Have you seen this?" Ann was bent over a color photo on her desk, and al- though it was early in the day, her French twist was already coming loose. Strands of graying blondish hair trailed across her forehead.

Jennie took the picture from her and sat in the seat across the way. "The Space Operations Center [SOC]," she read, "an artist's conception. A space station, to be permanently manned with a crew of eight to twelve, orbits the earth." She laughed and shook her head. "That'll be the day!"

"No, listen, they say they could have one of these up there by 1995 if the government funding holds out. Looks like a kid's creation from an Erector set, doesn't it?"

It did look bizarre, an assortment of knobs and tubes sitting on a shuttle-shaped central unit. It was gigantic, a regular small town floating in space. "I suppose it would serve the purpose, though." Jennie smiled politely, her mind not really on the conversation.

"What they have in mind is trying it out for a year, shifting crews halfway through. Of course, they'd be visited by other astronauts who'd come up to dock with them and carry out a variety of experiments."

"Like the Russians did." Jennie hadn't been the only one to marvel at the cosmonauts' staying up there for 256 days. The body changes over that period of time could be both debilitating and dangerous. Because you didn't use your muscles in anti-gravity, they started to atrophy after a while. Worse yet was the calcium loss as bone tissue began deteriorating. Counteracting that de- terioration was the prime goal of Jennie's research.

"I sure wouldn't want to be up there all that time," Ann muttered, signing the papers her frantic secretary shoved in front of her. "There's no shopping mall—not even a supermarket! And just think how your sex life would suffer!"

Jennie grinned at her incorrigible trainer. "It would be an utter disaster, I'm sure. Particularly for some of our guys. After six celibate months, I suspect some of them would turn in their flight badges for typewriters."

"I'd think they send up some of the married couples, wouldn't you? We've got four in the program right now, and if they're serious about this mission, they're going to have to accommodate to . . . well . . . to basic human emotions, right?"

"Sex in space?" Jennie laughed. "I can't imagine."

"You couldn't *do* very much, I wouldn't think—not floating around, anyhow." Ann finally looked up from her papers. "This is a silly conversation. Listen, I saw the postings earlier. I'm sorry, Jen. I thought you had it."

Jennie ran her fingers through her curls and sighed. "Frankly, I did, too. Now, why don't we get to work so I can be brilliant and get assigned to the next mission?"

Ann started to say something else but stopped herself. Jennie figured she was going to try to console her, and then thought better of it. Ann knew her too well to get soft with her. She probably thought Jennie was liable to break down and cry if anyone was too sympathetic. Jennie's main failing—in NASA terms—was that she took everything personally, whether it was criticism or praise. She was a damned good scientist and a tremendously hard worker, but she was feminine to the core. She knew Ann liked that about her, but others took the completely opposite view, which was that astronauts should have no tear ducts *or* feelings.

"Here are the PAM specs." Miraculously, Ann pulled the manual in question right out of the center of a pile of paper. "This is a typical cargo you might be asked to fly, so we're going to simulate the trajectories—launch and landing—and learn to work with the kind of computer software on board. It's different from the IUS and the *Centaur*, Jen—a whole new ball game."

"Good," Jennie said, forcing a smile as she got up and went to the door. "At least it'll keep my mind occupied. Hard work leaves no room at all for self-pity." Briskly, she started out into the corridor. But on her way to the mock control room, she was overcome with a terrible feeling of hopelessness. What was it? The conversation about married astronauts? She wasn't married. Or the space station? She had no chance of being assigned if she'd never flown a mission before. Or just the upcoming flight? She'd bombed out of that one. "Must be jinxed," she whispered under her breath as she came to her control room and opened the door.

To her surprise, the room was occupied. The trainers were generally careful about overbooking, so that astronauts were able to move smoothly from one work station to the next. But this room was filled with the top brass, and *that* was a real shocker.

She didn't want to interrupt these men, but her time on the control panel was at stake. They had plenty of conference rooms—why were they horning in on her territory?

"Jennie, come in, please, won't you?" offered Peter Reinhardt. His steely hair, always meticulously in place, reminded Jennie of a helmet.

"Am I interrupting something?" she asked pointedly.

"Guess we're interrupting *you*," Steve Akins, her immediate commander, joked. Captain Akins, a hard-line Navy man with a jaw of iron and blue-black hair that would never thin because Steve would command it not to, was one of the veteran astronauts, director of Flight Crew Operations. Despite the radical changes that had been going on for the past few years, Steve still hadn't gotten used to the idea that women in the program weren't just a figment of his overworked imagination. He had let Jennie know on more than one occasion that her outspoken manner was not acceptable—and wouldn't be until she turned into a man.

"I know you had this room until noon, Dr. Jacobs," said an Air Force colonel named Andersen, whom Jennie knew only by sight. He was something big in mission planning. "We've usurped it for a little discussion with you. Please, have a seat."

What is this all about? Jennie mused as she sat in one of the plastic chairs.

"We've been wondering how your research is coming, Jennie," Reinhardt went on. "What you're up to these days."

"I'm doing pretty well, actually," Jennie told him, her mind working furiously. Why would they be asking her all this if they weren't considering her? She was so nervous, she didn't even think about what she was saying. "I'm doing some treadmill tests to see what the effects of breakdancing in weightlessness might be." Then she laughed, but nobody else did. There was complete silence at the table until Peter Reinhardt made a noise that sounded something like a locomotive starting up.

"That Jennie, always joking. Uh, why don't you tell the group here what you're really doing?"

She wanted to kick herself, or at least swallow her tongue! No wonder these flatheads thought she was weird when she blurted out whatever came into her head.

"Of course, sir," she began quickly. "I'm testing to see how we might counteract loss of blood volume and fluid, increased vascular compliance, decreased endurance, impaired coordination, and, of course, calcium loss."

Steve Akins cut her off. "Jennie, you don't know much about heat-shield resistance, do you?"

She frowned, trying to keep her temper. "That's not

my field, of course, but I've been reading—"

"Have you been working with satellite deployment at all?" Andersen asked.

Now here was one where she could tell the truth and not get jumped on. "Yes, as a matter of fact, I—"

"I was wondering, Jennie," Reinhardt cut in, "whether Ann had given you much work with the guidance or instrumentation systems of the latest PAM module."

She counted to five, very slowly. "I was just beginning that today, sir," she told him humbly, gritting her teeth.

"That's right, gentlemen. We're keeping Dr. Jacobs from some important practice." Andersen got up and stalked to the door. He had dismissed her and gone on to something else, all within the space of a few seconds. "We certainly apologize for taking up your valuable time."

"We'll be talking with you again, Jennie," Reinhardt muttered.

Steve Akins gave her a look and walked out behind Andersen, leaving Jennie and Reinhardt alone in the control room.

"Ah, Jennie," Reinhardt began solicitously, "you know I think highly of you. But there's an attitude problem here. We realize you have a great deal to learn," he stated flatly, "but facts aren't everything. There's team spirit, there's patriotism, there's..." He stopped, perhaps realizing that he was sounding pretentious. "It's important to remember that we're all pulling for the same goal, and if that means abandoning your own work for a while, then so be it. You *do* understand that, don't you, Jennie?"

"I try to, sir," she said in as sincere a tone as she could muster. Actually, she itched to say something else outrageous, like the fact that her real interest was experimenting with extrasensory perception in space. She would have loved to see his jaw drop down to his nicely ironed socks. But she couldn't do it. NASA programmed the sense of humor out of all these guys, and she'd already gone too far.

"Don't give up the ship," was Reinhardt's cheery parting remark as he walked out the door.

"How can I give it up if no one will let me on board?" she moaned, alone now in the control room. She flipped the pages of her manual until she came to the description of the instrumentation system and sat herself down in front of the blank screen. "Telemetry formatter, RF transmitter, wide-band recorders—blah! Just because Dean Bradshaw can regurgitate this stuff in his sleep is no reason to expect everyone else to."

Willing herself not to think about Dean Bradshaw, she plugged in her software and watched the computer hum into action. So she didn't fit in. So she wasn't ready to fly—yet. She'd show them—all of them. And it wouldn't be long, either.

- 4 -

HER HOUSE SEEMED QUIETER, lonelier than usual tonight. She sat at the big bay window in the bedroom, sipping a glass of apple juice, watching the sky over the faraway water turn from gold to mauve to deep midnight blue. Like Dean's eyes, she thought.

Where was he? Had he gone out to celebrate with some of the guys? Could she have made the effort, gone along, had a good time despite herself? Probably not.

Dean. She wasn't even sure what he wanted from her. Maybe that kiss had been a spur-of-the-moment thing, like a quick flight to test out a new jet. As for the way she felt, it was mainly confusion, with a little anxiousness thrown in for good measure. When he was around, she couldn't think straight, and she didn't like that.

Wings sat beside her, purring quietly as Jennie stroked her soft patchwork-quilt fur. "What a day, huh, pal? Why do I keep batting zero?"

She had stripped off her no-nonsense day wear for a soft pink velour cowl-necked sweater and hot-pink crushed-silk pants. Somehow, even though no one was there to admire her outfit, it made her feel better about

51

herself, more womanly and more like a complete person. She loved being able to let down all the reserves, at least when she was alone.

"I could go see Susan and Jonesie," she murmured to the cat,. "but they'd suggest going out to drown my sorrows. And I don't want sympathy tonight. Or I could—"

She was interrupted by the sound of the doorbell, chiming loudly through the uncarpeted space. She'd saved all her pennies for a spectacular Oriental rug—a Pakistani beauty—and it sat proudly stage center in the living room. But since the rest of the place was skimpily, if tastefully, furnished, there was a great echo if you stood in the right place and sang a high G.

"Who's that?" she asked Wings, who jumped off the window seat and started for the door.

She might have expected anyone except Dean Bradshaw. He stood before her, a Yankees baseball cap in his hand, not smiling, looking rather somber and intent.

"Hi," she said. "How on earth...?"

"I got your address from personnel. Had no idea you lived so close."

"I told you that the other day."

"Oh."

The two of them just stared at each other. Jennie was becoming increasingly aware that Dean was giving her outfit the once-over. Her heart was pounding wildly in her chest. She was glad to see him but nervous, too. She was used to being able to predict her own behavior, but when he looked at her, she had no idea what she was capable of.

"Would you ... uh ... do you want to come in?" she asked finally.

"Sure." He followed her down the hall and into the living room, oblivious to everything but the woman walking barefoot in front of him. He didn't see the good oil paintings on the walls, or the Oriental carpet, or even the cat.

"Yow!" He leaped away after stepping on a bushy tail and causing Wings to screech at the top of her lungs.

"Watch it," Jennie laughed. "If you don't pass muster with Wings, you don't go anywhere in this place. It's like the army."

"I see," he said seriously, but his eyes were twinkling.

The skin around his eyes crinkled appealingly, and he had a prominent dimple in each cheek. She'd never noticed them before. His nose was angular, and his mouth was wide, curving upward naturally even when he wasn't smiling. It was funny, but seeing him here in her house made her see him more clearly, as if her surroundings brought out different aspects of him.

"I wanted to talk to you," he said quietly.

"Well, sit down. Talk," she offered, curling up on the brown velvet couch, the arms of which Wings had scratched into an interesting abstract pattern. She was flattered that he'd looked her up and terribly curious about his sudden interest in her. Her sudden interest in him was no small matter, either. The rush of emotion he caused in her made her tremble slightly.

"It was what I said this morning. I didn't mean it to sound arrogant."

"Then you didn't succeed," she told him honestly. "I'm afraid it sounded lousy."

"I know how much you want to fly, Jen, and—"

"How could you? You don't know anything about me." She tempered her statement with a smile.

"Let me start knowing." He got up from the chair and moved over next to her. She could smell his clean sea scent, and the heady aroma coursed through her too quickly. She had to get up, go somewhere, do something. She was too fidgety to sit in one place.

She jumped up to head for the kitchen. "Can I get you something to drink?" she asked. The light gold hairs on his hand shone in the lamplight as he reached for her.

"Sit down, will you?" he growled, startling her into compliance. He'd always been so careful with her, except for that day on the parachute jump—but that, of course, had been for effect, in front of the other guys.

"I'm sitting, I'm sitting!" She raised her hands in surrender and plopped back down on the sofa.

"I heard that the brass talked to you today. That's a good sign, at least," he offered in a softer tone. He was sitting so close, and yet he wanted to be closer. "You're going to get assigned soon, you know."

"Everyone is, eventually. I just wish I could have it now. It sounds selfish, I know, but I feel I deserve it now."

She narrowed her eyes at Dean, trying to see him as the enemy, as one of Them. It didn't work. Every time she was with him, Jennie sensed a split deep inside herself. She was in fierce competition with him; she resented his easy progress up the ladder of success; and if there was one thing she couldn't stand, it was being given a pat on the head and told her time would come. But on the other hand, she had the feeling she was melting, coming into orbit around him like the earth around the sun. He threw off heat, even at a distance.

He realized he was still holding the baseball cap, so he slapped it down on the end table. "Tell me, if you don't mind, how'd you get into this racket, anyway?"

"You want my life story?"

"I've got all night."

Forcibly ignoring the possible suggestiveness of his comment, she linked her hands behind her neck and sat there for a moment, gathering her thoughts. "Well," she began, "I've been flying a plane just for the heck of it since I was in college. My parents—they're both doctors—were convinced I was going to kill myself. My brother, Chris—he's a marine artist down in Florida—always cheered me on. I seemed to do all the things everyone expected Chris to do, you know? And he got into everything I refused to go in for. Then, Andy—he was my husband—was a flyer, too. So naturally..."

She didn't finish the sentence. It felt awkward to be talking about Andy.

"You're divorced?" he asked, leaning forward.

"Widowed. His T-38 went down two years ago."

Dean noticed that she'd kept her voice steady, but not so controlled that he couldn't hear the pain. "I'm sorry, Jennie. Really I am." He was silent for a moment, and when he spoke again, Jennie was grateful that he had the sensitivity to change the subject. "You know, it's strange. I had the same thing with my brother. Everything my folks wanted for me, Jim got. I truly believe they think that one day I'll give up this nutsiness and go to med school."

Jennie grinned. "You can never please them. I thought getting a Ph.D. would make all the difference to mine, but they just kept asking when I was going to have a baby. They still ask!" She chuckled a little. "I used to tell them I'd have a child only if I could give birth on the moon, but now I think, well, maybe someday." It was more complicated than that, actually. Andy hadn't wanted children; she had. Andy had won.

"You know," Dean said, getting up and walking to the window so that he wouldn't keep looking into her deep hazel eyes and feeling as if he were drowning, "I hope it doesn't make you uncomfortable or anything, but I've been watching you lately. You have more commitment than any twelve people in this program. Sometimes I see that look in your eye, and by gosh, if it doesn't remind me of me!" He laughed. "I wouldn't be surprised if you could do anything you set your mind to."

She licked her lips, listening to his words. He liked her for her hard work and for their similar attitudes. That was odd—Andy had seemed to admire all the things about her they *didn't* have in common. She leaned her head back on the sofa, feeling looser, more accepted.

"Thanks for your vote of confidence. It's still going to be hard, though. You work your butt off to learn a specialty, and then they insist you don't have the flight qualifications. Then, when you get those, you can't even use your specialty. You have to be the compleat Renaissance person but never buck authority. The only reason I keep banging my head against this wall is that I think space exploration is more important than Lewis and Clark—maybe even more important than Columbus. If we're going to leave any legacy to future generations, it's got to be a better knowledge of Earth and our universe. Who knows? We may even have to find them someplace else to live in case we blow it down here. And I want to be there—I want to be part of the solution."

She heard herself rambling and clapped a hand over her mouth. "Lord, how I do run on!"

She felt a hand lift hers from her lips and saw Dean leaning over her. As she closed her eyes, she felt the soft caress of his mouth along her forehead and eyebrows, like the delicate brush of starlight on a lake. Her stomach tightened as he worked his way down her cheek and found her eager mouth. She was ready for him.

They kissed for a long time, beginning a wonderful exploration with hands and tongues and lips. His huge hands encompassed her face, and she felt safe suddenly, and as if a great weight had been lifted off her shoulders. She was also trembling, her legs shaking involuntarily even as his hand crept down her neck to her soft breasts.

She gasped and drew away. "I . . . Dean . . . I'm really not . . ."

"I think you are. I think we both are. You remember the other day, how you were talking to me about first impressions?" He knelt by the side of the sofa and took her hands in his. "I knew this was right more than a year ago."

She pursed her lips and gave him a lopsided smile. "Well, in that case, you're a pretty slow study."

"You're right. Frankly, lady, I'm shy."

"Hmm, I might have guessed. But why is this hap-

pening to us now?" she persisted softly. She could feel
it from him, too, a growing flame that licked at the two
of them.

"We both opened our eyes at the same time, I suppose.
I held off too long, too long." His fingers traced the
contours of her face, memorizing each facet of it. So
lovely, so willing.

Jennie ached to kiss him again, but some part of her
felt terribly strange about her eagerness. Andy's picture
on the sideboard was a keen reminder of how long it had
been since she'd felt like this about a man. And with
Andy there hadn't even been all that much physical at-
traction. They were the best of friends and very loving,
but the chemistry was more H_2O than TNT. The feeling
she had now was positively volatile, as if she were a
bomb about to detonate.

The two of them stayed there, smiling at each other,
and for a brief moment Jennie was embarrassed that she'd
been jealous of his success. He seemed to have the ability
to shift her mood radically without appearing to do or
say anything at all. Or maybe it was the blinding excitement of his touch. She was still shaking a little, but
she tried to hide it. She couldn't let on that she had
wobbly knees, even if they were shaking so much she'd
have to be carried to the bedroom.

Jennie! She was shocked at herself for thinking that
way. After all, this was practically the first real conversation she'd ever had with the man, and already she was
thinking about their naked bodies, rolling and pitching,
joined together in an ecstasy of hot passion. This wasn't
like her at all! As a matter of fact, she couldn't remember
one time in her life when she'd wanted to drag a man
bodily into bed. Until now.

She clutched his head to her breast and felt his hands
slide up under the soft fabric of her velour top. It would
be so easy to let it happen, to give in to this wonderful,
stupefying feeling. His hands were warm, slightly cal-

loused. They massaged her back and sides, working the soft, alabaster skin like moist clay. He kissed her randomly—now on her breast, now on her inner arm. She tingled and burned, craving more.

"Dean, wait. I can't think!"

"Don't bother." The words were muffled against her.

"It's too soon for us. Please. I want this, too, but I'm too confused right now." But she held on to him, giving the lie to her own words.

As he looked up, she noticed the gentle smile in his eyes. "Jennie, let's go away for a weekend. Get some sun, some time to ourselves. Time to get acquainted. Lady, I want to know you inside out."

She was astounded to feel tears stinging her eyes, and she blinked them away rapidly. It was his intensity, the fervent way he came to her, wanting her. Nobody had ever treated her that way. So why was she so frightened of her own feelings? Why was she holding back?

"It sounds lovely. I'll . . . Let me think about it."

"Too much thinking is bad for your happiness quotient, you know," he teased her lightly. "Sometimes it's best to go with the flow. When you really want something—when *I* know I want something, anyhow—I don't question."

She pursed her lips, sorry that she was being so analytical. "Well, I do. I guess that's where we're different."

"Jennie," he said softly, his hands massaging her shoulders, making her loose and pliant, "don't ponder this. Just let it happen." He kissed her again, his lips easing her own open.

After several moments, he reluctantly got to his feet and, as if it was too difficult to look at her, turned around and started for the front hall. Wings padded quickly behind him. The night, balmy with the pungent smell of the bay, washed in through the door when he opened it.

"See you in the morning, Jen," he said.

"Good night. Hey!" she called to Wings, who had promptly trotted outside behind Dean. She scooped up the struggling cat in her arms, but it was impossible to hold her. With a leap, Wings landed on Dean's left shoulder.

"I think you made a conquest." Jennie smiled, folding her arms and leaning on the doorjamb.

"I hope I made two," he told her solemnly, detaching the cat and handing her back to Jennie. Their hands touched under the velvet fur. "I'd better get out of here before I start looking at you again." He leaned over and gave her a chaste little kiss on her cheek, then strode to his car and got in. He was out of sight before she could turn around.

His baseball cap lay on the table where he'd left it, and she hugged it to her face, closing her eyes tightly. "I think something's happening," she said aloud. "And I think I like it. Just wish I could be sure."

She turned out the light and sat for a long, long time in the dark, staring out at the night sky.

"Okay, watch this, Jennie. There's nothing to it." Steve Akins sat inside the small module and activated the remote manipulator system. A clawlike arm projected from the simulator, blindly grasping at air.

"My nephew has a toy Jeep like this," Jennie commented. "He pushes buttons, and the thing climbs a sand dune. Then he turns it over and yells with glee." She shook her head as Steve handed her the controls. "It's like rubbing your head and patting your belly at the same time."

"You'd better catch on; this is important." He guided her hand as she attempted to maneuver the claw to pick up a bolt and put it in place. The bolt dropped through a hole in the floor.

"Drat!"

"Again." So she tried again. This time she made it.

Steve had been watching her all day, and she was exhausted. It was one thing to work as hard as she ever had and have no time for her own research, but in the past week they'd thrown stuff at her she hadn't looked at since she was a rookie. Stuff they only concentrated on right before a flight.

However, she wasn't really hopeful anymore. There were five other mission specialists more qualified than she, and they'd all been given the same amount of attention this week as she had. It wasn't usual for a trainer to follow you around all day like a private detective, and it grated on Jennie's sense of independence. But what could you do? The life of an astronaut was grin-and-bear-it, then tell the press it was "top choice, grade-A, and thanks for asking." Even when they started you on the cruel and unusual tasks like riding the centrifuge or staying inside a closed canvas oxygen bag for half an hour, you were never supposed to complain—just beg for more.

"All right, that'll do it for today," Steve said, grimacing as she swung the arm high in the air and it jerked wildly back and forth. "Try to book some more time here with Ann, would you?" he told her as he got up and started for the door. "You need it."

"Yes, sir." She brought the arm back to zero position and secured it in its cradle. She felt grouchy and insecure, as if she were always walking on needles. Maybe she was being told she just didn't cut the mustard. Maybe they were planning to ditch her. But how could they? She was good—just inexperienced. Maybe she didn't have the qualifications that Dean had, or any of the rest of the crew that had been selected, but with time she could get them. She was sure of that.

Reluctantly, she acknowledged that part of her antsiness had to do with not having seen Dean for a week now. He'd been plugging away for hours on end, closeted with the top training staff day and night. He'd been telephoning regularly, allowing them to get better acquainted, but their late-night phone calls just weren't satisfying. How could they be when what they both wanted was something tangible?

"Are you still awake?" he'd asked last night at about midnight.

"Are you still alive?" she'd countered, dragging the phone into bed with her and shoving Wings off the pillow.

"Barely. I don't know, they seem to be trying to ascertain whether I'm just human or might qualify for superhuman. It's exhausting."

She listened to the low rumble of his voice and remembered the feel of his lips as they pressed against hers, his breath warming her. "Well, tell them off. Open your mouth and say stop," she counseled.

"Like you, you mean? No, thanks. I'll do my work like a good Boy Scout and worry later about the aftereffects on my psyche. If I've got a psyche left to affect!"

Jennie laughed, certain he was right—that he knew the way to act and she didn't. They'd never let her fly unless she came off like a pro in every situation. Unless she came off like a Dean Bradshaw.

She thought about that conversation as she walked out into the bright morning sunlight. Let's analyze this, she thought. What was holding her back? She was dedicated, but the brass had its doubts. She was worthy, but they seemed to think she was . . . an alien. An alien with the right stuff, but a weirdo nonetheless. She *did* find the routine work extremely routine; she always had. Some of the guys at the center got all hot and bothered about OVM's and RMS's, but she couldn't muster any enthusiasm at all. Space to her was science's broad new frontier, ultimately a realm to inhabit, a place to call a new home. There was, however, a lot of boring stuff to learn before you reached that frontier. For instance, one thing Jennie had never wanted to learn was to unstop an antigravity toilet, but this afternoon she was going to.

"Wait up a second! Dr. Jacobs, is that you?"

She turned and shaded her eyes, squinting into the sun, but she couldn't make out the face. There was something familiar about him, about the way he stood and moved.

"Well, can't say it's been a long time, can I?" he asked when he was within a few yards of her.

"Dr. Bradshaw. Jim Bradshaw?" She looked at him curiously, imagining his brother beside him. If she hadn't known better, she never would have suspected the two men were related. "What are you doing here?"

"I was looking for Dean, but they tell me he's locked up with some machine and won't be out till next Friday."

"That's what they do with people in training. It's like quarantine." Jennie laughed. "I just wish the disease were catching," she added more softly.

"You didn't get tapped, huh?" he asked in a sympathetic voice.

"Not this time. Guess they figure I'm too green. So what *are* you doing in Clear Lake again? I thought you had a New York practice that kept you busier than an astronaut." They began walking together toward one of the reflecting pools. A darning needle slipped across the water, making a phosphorescent rainbow of blues and greens right beside them.

"That's true, but fortunately, I have a colleague who helps out in a pinch. One of my patients is having a heart transplant down here at the medical center, and the surgeon asked me to come along on a consult. I'll be around for a couple of weeks."

"Great," Jennie said politely. "I don't think you're going to see much of your brother, though."

"Well, in that case, I'll need some other kind of companionship. How about you?" He stopped and tilted his head, squinting down at her, his chestnut hair highlighted by the blazing sun, his brown eyes demanding an answer.

"I'm not exactly on vacation myself," she said with a sigh. "But I'd certainly be happy to show you around."

"I can't wait. Shall we get started?"

Jennie liked the man, genuinely felt comfortable with him. He was so easy to talk to. And Dean *was* tied up. He might be relieved if she agreed to play tour guide for his brother.

"I was just going to the commissary to grab a sandwich, and you're certainly welcome to come, but I have a very full afternoon and—"

"Why don't I pick you up after you're through with work, and we can have dinner? I should be getting back to the hospital about now."

"That sounds fine." Dinner with Jim would be nice, of course, but she wondered if it would just make her more lonely. It was his brother she longed to be with, after all. She could play the gracious hostess without blinking an eye, but her heart wouldn't be in it. This wasn't the man who caused her breath to get shorter and her arms to ache with the desire to embrace him.

But, she reminded herself, there was no reason for her to get all upset. This was a simple dinner with a nice, charming guy—not a romantic interlude with the one who ignited a raging fire within her. To compare the two would be like equating apples and oranges.

"Why don't you meet me in front of Building four at six-thirty? If I'm late, you can—"

"Await you with eager anticipation," Jim said lightly, resting a hand on her arm. "I'll be early, probably."

They said their good-byes beside the pool, and as Jennie walked toward the cafeteria, she was acutely aware of her own sense of disappointment. Why couldn't she be having dinner with Dean instead?

The truth of the matter was, she found it hard to concentrate on anything except Dean these days, despite the fact that she hadn't seen him lately. She was beginning to think there was more to her feelings than simple desire, and that made her uneasy. She had always wanted things to be neat and straightforward, but now she seemed to be tempting fate to scramble her emotions and tumble her into the middle of an erupting volcano.

- 5 -

JENNIE TOOK DEAN'S brother to a little Tex-Mex restaurant she particularly liked. It was a homey, ranch-style place, with sprawling long tables and bowls of chili sauce so strong it could remove paint—just how Jennie liked it.

She had a feeling it wasn't Jim's style, though. He talked about a classy little Mexican restaurant in downtown Manhattan's Soho as though it were Mecca, and he complained about the noise and smoke. Well, Jennie figured, they just weren't on the same wavelength.

But then, over coffee, they got into a conversation about her childhood in Wisconsin, her brother Chris's painting, and her work, and she sensed Jim's genuine interest. There was no question about it: Jim was a charmer. He listened terrifically well and complimented her every chance he got. According to him, she was the Venus de Milo and Einstein rolled up in one woman, with a little Margaret Mead thrown in for good measure.

"Now that's a line if I ever heard one!" she exclaimed as he sent yet another verbal bouquet her way.

"Jennie, I'm crushed! I wouldn't know a line if I

tripped over it." He put his hands over his heart, feigning hurt.

"Sure, tell me another." She laughed and drank the dregs of her coffee. "It's incredible how unalike you and Dean are," she added, feeling slightly guilty that, although she was with Jim, she was thinking about how lovely it would be to be with his brother.

"You're right. He's the one with the deep soul. I'm just a superficial cad." Jim shrugged.

"Oh, I wouldn't say that." She wanted to pump him for more information about Dean but felt that he would tell her what he chose to in his own good time.

"No, it's true. He's got a kind of substance I admire. When he wants something, he'll go to the ends of the earth for it. I give up rather easily—always have. But," he added as he got up and swept her out of her chair, "I bet I have more fun. Shall we?"

They drove back to her place in his rented car, talking freely, as if they had known each other for years. He parked in her driveway and looked at her.

"This has been great, Jim. I'm glad we did it." Jennie smiled warmly, extending her hand.

"Shall we trip the light fantastic tomorrow night? I never did get that dance out of you." He wouldn't let go of her hand.

"Oh, no, you're not roping me into that one."

"Dinner, then. Maybe we can dig my brother out of his trench."

"I sincerely doubt that," she said regretfully. "Look, let's talk later in the week, okay?"

"How can I argue with an astronaut?" He laughed. "I should know by now how impossible that is. So I'll give you time—till tomorrow."

She gave him a disparaging glance and got out of the car.

"Say, Jennie, do you mind if I use your phone? I really ought to check in with the hospital."

"Of course." She walked to her front door, and he followed close behind her, waiting quietly until she'd opened it.

"Go right ahead." She waved at the phone in the hall and stooped to pick up Wings. Jim just stood there. "Oh, sorry," she said. "I'm sure you'd like some privacy." She started to go into the living room. "Dial one first for Houston."

"Thanks."

She was perfectly awful about eavesdropping on other people's conversations. Chris had started her off on this when he was a ten-year-old bundle of mischief and she was eight and thought everything he did was miraculous. Now, of course, she hated him for it. She made every attempt to turn off her ears and go about her business, but words and attitudes always filtered out to her.

She went into the kitchen to putter around and mercifully was able to hear only muffled words. What she did hear, however, didn't sound like a serious discussion about a patient. There was a lot of laughter and many long pauses. And then, as she came out to the living room again, she distinctly heard the word *sweetheart*. Did New York physicians use endearments on everyone to be chic or something? It was very odd.

He hung up and waited for her, evidently attempting to prolong his visit. "Tomorrow?" he said.

She simply smiled and saw him to the door.

"I'll try to get Dean tomorrow, too," he added.

"Right. Well, good night. And thanks again."

"Thank *you*." He turned and looked at her. "Why don't *I* ever stumble across gems like you?"

She winked, shaking her head. "Gems like me you have to dig for. Not everyone has the patience."

She went to bed that night uneasy and uncertain. What she'd said was true. It took patience to get to know her. Did Dean have that kind of perseverance?

* * *

When she saw the event posted on the bulletin board, she knew she had to go and watch. A big mistake, she told herself sternly. Yet, it was a beautiful day for a flight, and the man was certainly a skilled pilot. Besides, it was about time she got over the feeling that her heart was going to stop every time she saw a small jet take off.

Dean's flying the T-89 this afternoon, was the refrain that ran through her head from the moment she saw the notice to the time she finished her work for the day and set out for the airfield, several miles away from the center. He didn't know she was coming—that was just as well.

"Look who's here!" Rob Callahan, one of the mission specialists assigned to the next flight with Dean, was waiting at the hangar for them to bring the plane around. Rob was a pixie of a man, an Army lieutenant who, at thirty-four, had logged more flight hours than all but one of the pilot astronauts. His speciality was metallurgical engineering, which made him very attractive to the various companies interested in exploiting the commercial aspects of space exploration. Rob was brilliantly red-haired and florid, and when he twitched his thin mustache, he looked something like a ferret. His wife, Nancy, loved to torment him about the thing and threatened to shave it off one night while he was sleeping.

"What are you doing here?" he asked when she just stood there, white-faced and anxious, staring at the jet as if it were an atomic bomb.

"I've heard a lot about this trainer," she said, snapping out of her reverie. "Thought it might be interesting to see Dean take it up."

And at that moment, Dean appeared from under one wing. He had a smudge of grease on his face, and it gave him the rakish look of a pirate who'd just captured a particularly juicy king's ransom with no thought to the danger involved. He stared at Jennie, then came toward her. She felt dizzy, and she didn't know whether it was due to his nearness or to the fact that everything inside her screamed to tell him to chuck the assignment and walk away *now*.

"Want to take a spin with me?" he asked casually.

She smiled; this particular plane had only one seat. "I'll pass this time. Can't stand cramped quarters," she told him. A silence stretched between them.

Finally, Rob cleared his throat and said, "Well, I think I'll look over your flight plan, Dean. Gotta make sure I don't lose you up there."

Jennie winced. She knew all too well how a pilot could get "lost" in a tester.

"You really want to watch this?" Dean asked her when Rob had walked off toward the flight controller's booth from which he and other NASA personnel would be clocking Dean's somersaults through the heavens.

"No, of course I don't. But I have to," Jennie said. "Hell, it'll be good for me. Kind of like a cold shower." She paused. "Make that a hundred cold showers. By the way, I brought you this. You left it on my coffee table." She held out the Yankees cap.

"You hold on to that for me. I don't need it right now."

He grinned and gave her a quick kiss, leaving a spot of grease on her nose. He made a futile attempt to wipe it off. "You're a marked woman. Guess there's nothing much you can do about that."

"Dean, I wish . . ." No, she wouldn't allow herself to say she was worried sick, that she didn't want him to go. Work was work, after all. And what did the statistics say? More people slipped in bathtubs and cracked their heads open than died in tester jets. Something like that.

"I know what you wish." He gave her a broad grin. "But delayed gratification is important in this life. How about a bottle of champagne at my place tonight? Or beer if you'd prefer. Or anything?" His words were an open invitation, and she suddenly knew she would accept that invitation. She wanted him, wanted him badly.

"You're on."

"Hey, Dean!" Jeff Davis yelled. "Are we taking this baby up, or just assuming she works 'cause she looks so sweet?"

Dean raised his arm in a military salute, and as it came down he grabbed Jennie around the waist and gave her a hug. "Now you get to see some real acrobatics. Go sit somewhere so you won't fall down, okay?" he added, tender compassion in his voice. He seemed to know how hard this was for her.

"Jen, I just want to tell you that more people die in their own bathtubs than—"

"I know, I know!" Her laugh bordered on hysteria, and she walked away as quickly as she could.

Dean crawled inside the tiny hatch, adjusting his oxygen mask and helmet. The ground crew helped him taxi the plane outside into the radiant sunshine. Jennie clenched the baseball cap between her hands, holding it like a lifeline, and closed her eyes briefly. Then she forced them open. She had to look.

The sleek silver trainer with its tiny jet engine moved gracefully, like a shark cutting through water. There was hardly anything to it—just a thin body and a couple of sweep wings. They all said it was the best, though, and better practice for a pilot than any other craft. If you could keep this bucking bronco under control, you could handle anything.

The plane taxied to the end of the runway, then started speeding faster and faster, a blur of light along the sand. Jennie held her breath for the takeoff. In her mind's eye, she could see the airspeed mach indicator climbing.

The wheel flaps lifted, and he was airborne, sailing off into the azure sky as though the plane were some little boy's kite, up for a whirl on a clear day. Then the distance between him and the earth seemed to shift. The plane nosed down, and suddenly it was on its side.

"Damned showoff has to start out like a maniac," Jennie muttered under her breath. She realized that she

hadn't breathed since he'd taken off, and she forced some
air into her lungs, inhaling painfully.

The plane came out of its curve and started up, so high
that within seconds it was out of sight. But then, through
a cloud bank, she saw its tail once again, spinning madly,
over and over. She was angry with herself, an experienced
amateur pilot, for feeling this way. It was one thing for a
layman to be terrified, but it was curtains for an expert.
Once you had fear, they said, the fear had you.

Will I feel this way on a shuttle flight? she wondered
suddenly, never taking her eyes off that careening bird
high above her. Because, if so, I should quit now. She
forced herself to concentrate on the plane, to memorize
the maneuvers and detail them in her head. She imagined
Dean's hand on the stick, *in charge* of the roll and pitch.
For godsake, he knew what he was doing.

But then, so had Andy. Skill wasn't the only factor
involved in success; luck was, too.

The sky was so clear, so open. The silver plane sliced
through the blue surface like a fish breaking water, and
then Jennie saw it start upward. A plane like this could
glide through the heavens even faster than a T-38; it
could ride along effortlessly at Mach 1.4 straight, Mach
1.8 in a dive. It was Dean's job to take her through her
paces, and he did, handling her as if he were an experienced horseman showing a thoroughbred. Like a cowboy, Jennie thought with an ironic smile. Now he urged
her forward, and he was only a blur; now he pitched her
on her side and flew along like a lopsided eagle. It was
evident that he was in complete control.

At that point Jennie began to relax and admire what
he was doing. His was a beautiful display of the power
of high technology, an amazing exhibit of man working
together with machinery. Without the man, the machine
would have been static, useless. Yes, Jennie grinned, the
guy was good. He was exciting.

She was caught unaware when, suddenly, the T-89

seemed to stop in midair. The next second, it was plummeting toward the earth, coming straight down, rocketing for the ground with a death wish so consuming it could never be turned back. Her heart pounded crazily, and she started running, not even knowing where she was going. It struck her that if she lost this man, she would lose the renewed hope that had entered her life. If she could have put up her hands, blocked the plane's flight, stopped it with her own body, she would have done it.

"Dean!" she cried uselessly, running out onto the field. She felt someone come after her and grab her, but she was oblivious to his soothing words.

And then, abruptly, the nose of that suicidal bird turned up jauntily. The plane evened out and started its leisurely descent to earth. It came down like a feather, softly speeding across its lovely azure backdrop. It turned one more somersault, then circled the area for a landing. Dean brought it in clean, stopping on a dime, and all Jennie heard was the hum of blood in her ears matching that of the high-tech engines.

He lifted the Plexiglas shield of the cockpit and gave the thumbs-up sign. Dimly, in the background, Jennie heard the people in the flight-control booth cheering.

"Hey, he's really something, isn't he?" Rob Callahan, who had been the one who stopped her dash onto the runway, was thumping her back and pounding his thigh with his free hand.

Still, she couldn't speak, nor could she when Dean walked over to her and casually took her arm. "Not bad for a little jobber. What's next?"

She wanted to hit him! The man was so arrogant, so totally sure of himself. He knew exactly how good he was, and he loved having the rest of the world know, too.

"Next," she said as calmly as she could, "you have to subject yourself to a death-defying ride in a red Ford pickup. And this time, *I'm* driving."

"Okay by me, lady, since I got a lift here from the center. Let me just log in my notes." His face seemed about to split in two, he was grinning so broadly.

They took her truck to Shoreacres. There was an unspoken bond between them, a decision they had made simultaneously without any need for discussion. Jennie drove in silence, feeling the warmth from the man beside her. He was quiet, too, almost a different person from the one who had emerged, triumphant, from the man-eating shark that had torn through the heavens just a brief time ago.

"You remembered the turn," he commented when she started for his house without any direction.

"Pocahontas, my brother used to call me." Jennie smiled. It was the first time they'd spoken in an hour. "All you have to do is show me something once. I catch on."

"That's nice to know," he murmured.

She glanced over at him as she pulled the truck up close to the house and turned off the engine. What exactly had he meant by that? The depths of his eyes contained so much, it was hard to filter out one message among the others.

"The champagne isn't cold yet. I never like to ice it before I'm certain I'll be around to drink it." Dean chuckled as he unlocked the door and ushered her inside.

She was immediately on guard. "Not funny."

"No? Guess not. It's a reality, though. Did your husband put his on ice before he went up?"

She gasped and moved away from him. "That's a horrible thing to s——" she began, but he grabbed her arm and pulled her forcibly against him.

"Jen, you're time-traveling again. Most of the time you're in the present," he said firmly, his face only inches from hers, "but then you jump back a couple of years and your eyes go all blurry and you're simply not there anymore. What I want to know before you and I go any further is, what time is it now—past or present?"

"Oh, Lord." She sighed deeply. "I'm here with you now, Dean. Really, I am." And she suddenly knew she meant it. Even as he took her in his arms and brought his mouth down on hers, she understood that watching him fly had done something to her. This afternoon, she had given up Andy's ghost and put it to rest. She wanted—no, needed desperately—to move on.

His lips drove her crazy, moving from her mouth down to the soft white skin beneath her right ear. He whispered indeciferable words to her, both reassuring and mysterious. They spoke of tenderness but also of determination. Now that they were here, together, she knew he wouldn't let her go.

She wrapped her arms around his slim waist and clung to him, letting him move her backward toward the oak sideboard that stood on one side of the living room. He held her there and kissed her again, easing his hands down along her back, down toward the ripe curve of her buttocks. She was melting, loose in his arms, giving way under the insistent pressure that radiated from him like heat from a fireplace. He molded her in his grasp, drawing her to him.

"Jennie, I want you so badly," he murmured.

"Yes," she said. And that was all she needed to say.

They moved together toward the floor, sinking into the plush beige carpet, their bodies linked as though they could not be separated. His tongue ran along the delicate bones that highlighted her jaw, and she shivered with delight. Suddenly, she couldn't wait any longer. She reached for him, knowing he was ready. The long, hard length of him pulsed under her hand. Carefully, she undid his belt and unzipped his jeans, eager for all that he clearly intended to bestow on her.

"Do you want to stay here, sweetheart?" he asked. "Or would you prefer the satin sheets?"

"Who needs sheets?" she murmured into his T-shirt.

And smiling gently, she proceeded to undress him, relishing the sight of his tanned, smooth body, perfect except for two scars on his left shoulder and one down below that testified to a long-ago appendectomy.

"How old?" she asked, kissing the scar.

"I was eight. Damned thing nearly exploded before Ma could get me to the hospital. She didn't believe in hospitals, you see."

"A fanatic, huh?"

"Just like me. Never pay attention to inconsequential details when you can rejoice in the really important things. Like you."

He rolled her over onto her back and worked her maroon, French-cut T-shirt out of her pants. Underneath, she was wearing a lacy black bra that plunged becomingly between her full, rounded breasts. Dean laughed with surprise. "The real you. I like that. The lady comes to work dressed like a mechanic, but under that disguise lurks the seductress."

Jennie blushed and tried to move away, but he pinned her in place, his powerful arms holding her steady. "Not really. My next-door neighbor Susan gave it to me for my birthday and insisted I wear it one day a week. She'd about given up on my sex life."

"Well, next time you see her, you can tell her she has nothing further to worry about." With that, he whipped off her clay-colored drawstring pants, revealing the matching black bikini beneath. The rest of their clothes were off without her even knowing it, and then they stared at each other, marveling in the nakedness that united them.

Jennie felt her excitement rising as he nuzzled her nipple, bringing it to a peak of tender delight. Her flat stomach was his next object of attention, and he ran his tongue around her navel, cherishing it slowly, tantalizingly, before going on to her slender thighs.

It had been so long! She scarcely remembered what

it was like to feel a man's touch, and she could hear herself breathing roughly. All thought left her mind except being with him, pleasing him, taking pleasure from him. As if he sensed her gradual rediscovery of her sensuality, he slowed his approach, showering feathery kisses on her, leaving her body free for his adoration. Jennie reached for him, but he shook his head, pulling just out of her grasp.

"Let's take our time, sweetheart," he counseled her softly. "I want this to last forever."

And he tried his hardest to make sure it did. They rolled together, their limbs entwined, sharing a closeness that didn't demand immediate reward. Their hands in each other's hair, they let their lips and tongues speak for them in the process of exploring and pleasuring.

Just when she thought she could stand the torturous excitement no longer, he parted her thighs. He slipped inside easily, effortlessly, and it was like starting again. Her hazel eyes opened wide in awe, and she trembled, holding him against the onslaught of her internal storm.

He let her lead him, hoping that she would never stop calling his name, that she would always have this look of wild abandon on her face.

"When they go down too deep in subs, you know," he whispered, drawing away just enough to make her gasp, "they experience a euphoria that blinds them to everything else. It's called rapture of the deep. Same thing up there in the shuttle. If you don't watch out, you get space rapture. But I'm having it here, right here on earth."

And then he joined with her again, in a passionate dance that moved faster and stronger until the last moment, when she cried out and held him, then waited for him. He was there soon after, the expression on his face one of enormous tenderness and joy.

They were both panting and exhausted, yet neither wanted to stop. Within minutes, he was kissing her again.

They held on to each other, sometimes dozing, sometimes waking just to look at the other's sleeping, relaxed face. It grew darker, but the moon shone in on them, illuminating the room and the ecstasy they had found in each other. It was nearly ten when they wandered into the bedroom together, slipping between the cool sheets and hugging each other close.

"Hey, the champagne!" Dean started to get up, but Jennie held him in a way that informed him quite definitely that he was not to leave.

"Don't want any now," she murmured.

"Want something else?" He grinned.

"I wouldn't mind."

He rolled her on top of him, holding her suspended before lowering her gently so that her soft breasts just touched the golden hairs of his chest.

"Turn out the light, mister," she whispered. "And get ready for the ride of your life."

They didn't sleep much that night.

- 6 -

JENNIE AWAKENED FIRST and, propping herself on an elbow, looked down at the man beside her. So still, so peaceful, practically smiling in his sleep. It wasn't anything like the up-and-at-'em mornings she'd had with Andy. Her husband had been a positive fanatic about jumping out of bed and starting his exercise regime, even on Sundays. She hadn't thought much about it then, but now she realized they never made love in the mornings because he couldn't spare the time.

Time. What a lovely thing it was, Jennie mused, shifting her weight so as to be closer to Dean. She'd been rushing around nearly all her life, both personally and professionally, because she didn't know any other way. Last night, she'd learned a very important lesson about herself. She wanted to luxuriate in a man; she wanted the very essence of him to permeate her bones. What she'd had with Andy had been good for her way back then, but it wouldn't be now. Times had changed. Jennie had changed. Yes, indeed.

Stop jumping the gun, Jennifer, she cautioned herself. One-night stands, no matter how extraordinary, do not a relationship make. But she knew that Dean had been as affected by what had happened as she was. There was no denying that he had wanted her intensely. At one point, maybe around midnight, he hadn't been able to stop kissing her. He'd kissed every inch of her body and then, slowly, more carefully, as though he were polishing fine silver, he had started again. And she had loved every minute of it.

But there was more to it than even that. She'd been at least subconsciously aware of Dean's presence for the past three years, and now, almost without trying, she seemed to understand him, his habits, his whims. Despite herself, she *did* know something about him. She didn't have to be told that he'd sleep with the window open, that he never touched the air conditioner. She knew, by instinct, that he didn't snore and that he hardly moved when he was asleep. When he did things, he did them seriously—including making love.

She liked his bedroom. As she lay there, she watched the hazy morning light trace its slow path around the corners, hitting each shiny oak piece: an armoire topped with a stag's head, a dresser with an elaborate carved mirror, and—of all things—a canopy bed, minus the canopy. Interesting that someone who loved everything modern, whose house was the epitome of high-tech chic, should decorate as though he were living in the last century. It said a lot about him.

She traced his brow with one gentle finger. He stirred and reached for her, still asleep. But when she kissed an eyelid, it fluttered open. He looked up at her, grinning happily.

"Hello, lady." Dean pulled her over so that her head nestled in the crook of his arm.

"Hello yourself." She leaned over and kissed him on the forehead.

"That's all I get?"

"Oh, well, I guess I can do a little better." She pressed

her mouth down on his, and it opened eagerly, seeming to devour hers. When he finally let her go, she sighed happily. "Say, do you mind if we stop at my place so I can feed Wings? She's going to be extremely upset that her routine's been disturbed."

"No problem."

Jennie kissed his bicep and draped a leg over one of his, feeling the hard muscle beneath her contract and relax. "You know, I have a killer day—classes, plus briefing, plus simulator—and I'm not even dreading it."

"That's what a little affection will do for you. Sure you don't want to play hooky? We could call in sick."

She turned over and looked at him in horror. "And you in training for a mission! You have to be out of your mind. There'd be at least fifteen barracudas ready to replace you if you were merely late. Speaking of which . . ." She threw the light sheet off him and started yanking him by one foot. "Move it, cowboy."

"Only if you'll promise we can take this trainer up again tonight." He glanced down meaningfully at a certain part of his anatomy.

"That's the one that never runs out of fuel, right?" she teased.

"You got it." He ran his hands up her leg, and she turned to him in delicious agony.

"Dean, we can't now."

"But you want to?"

"Do you have to ask? Tonight, cowboy." She squirmed out of his grasp and staggered toward the bathroom. "And I want lots of time with you. Let's just hope your brother doesn't show up at a particularly interesting moment."

"Jim?" Dean raised himself on one elbow. "Now why should you mention him?"

She whipped her head around, puzzled. "Because he's here. At the hospital. Didn't you know? He had a patient transferred down here for an operation at the medical center."

Dean was out of bed in a minute, his powerful body seeming to take up most of the room. "You're kidding!"

She shook her head. "You mean he never got hold of you? We had dinner together the other night, for heaven's sake. He said he was going to call you the next morning."

Dean's handsome face clouded. "What do you mean, you had dinner?"

"Dinner—as in food, as in eating. Dean, what's the matter with you?" She leaned against the doorframe for a second, aware of Dean's barely concealed anger. "He said he was going to call you, but you know how hard it is to reach you these days."

"Jennifer," he said quietly, "I know Jim's a great guy, but I really wish you wouldn't see him again."

Her face broke into a disbelieving smile. "I never would have imagined you had a jealous bone in your body. I'm flattered."

"I'm serious, Jennie."

She put a hand on his arm and shook it lightly. "Your brother, in case you don't know, is a perfectly charming person who's a stranger in a strange town. I thought you'd be delighted if I showed him around while you were busy."

"No. I mean, it was nice of you, but, no, I'm not delighted."

"What is it with you two?" she asked. When he was silent, she said, "I think I have a right to know. I make friends—male or female—wherever I find them, Dean. And nobody tells me otherwise unless there's a very good reason for it."

He turned away from her, and as he walked back toward the bed, she was reminded of an angry panther. "Years ago," he began slowly, "I was in love—or thought I was—with this woman named Marilyn. We were both pretty young and pretty silly, and I suppose it was all for the best that we split up. But while we were engaged, Jim came home from med school. He appeared on the scene one day, and Marilyn fell for him like an anchor going down fast. I never saw anything like it. She dropped me like I had the plague."

Jennie frowned. "Did...uh...did Jim encourage this?"

"I don't know. We never really discussed it. At any rate, they didn't stay together very long," he said tersely. "Of course," he added, "Jim never was with any one woman for very long."

"Well, maybe it was all for the best," she said sensibly even as she wondered why two brothers would fail to talk about something so important. "After all, you said you thought she wasn't the right person for you," Jennie offered. "Maybe he didn't think—"

"It was a lousy thing to do," Dean growled.

"I agree. But it was a long time ago. Why didn't you ever talk to Jim about it?" she asked, thinking she already knew the answer. Dean had taken three years to approach her; he wasn't the kind of man who blurted out his feelings on the spot.

"In my own way, I tried. He shrugged it off, said it was all her doing."

"Did he ever do anything like that again?"

"Well, not exactly, no, but—"

"There you are. Dean, I think you're overreacting." She smiled and rumpled his hair.

"Maybe. Maybe not." He eased himself away from her, not liking the idea that suddenly she might be at the center of a family dispute. "I guess I'm exaggerating. I have a tendency to do that. Like about you." He came back toward her, grabbing her roughly and bringing her tightly against his massive chest. "I think you're probably the best thing that ever happened to me. Hey, lady." Dean's hands began to work their way down her shoulders, then found the path that led to her perfectly rounded breasts. She shuddered with pleasure. "Remember I asked if you'd like to go away with me? I'm asking again."

"You can't now. You're in training." She couldn't think when his hands set her on fire this way, every nerve ending tense with anticipation of the next brush of his fingers.

"I can get a weekend. We'll take a T-33 and steal off into the night. How about it?"

She grinned and nodded her agreement. "As a matter of fact, I've been meaning to go down to Florida to see my brother and sister-in-law. They've got this great houseboat off one of the Keys. We could go there."

"I want you alone." He pressed close, and she felt the intention of his words in a potently physical way.

"Don't sweat it, cowboy." She grinned, pulling away and starting for the shower. "They're not like real relatives. If you want, they leave you completely alone after you've said hello. Anyhow, you'd like Chris and Molly. Timmy's terrific, too. He's their seven-year-old."

Dean made a face and shrugged, then threw up his hands, sensing that this was the best he would get from her right now. He wondered if the conversation about Jim had upset her as much as it had him. "You win. We fly to Florida. This afternoon I'll find out what my schedule is."

After they dressed, he poured them tall glasses of grapefruit juice, which they drank in the truck on the way to Jennie's house. She dropped some crunchies in a bowl for Wings, apologized profusely to the cat, then ran back to the truck.

They were only slightly late for work. They left the truck at Parking Lot 2 beside Dean's car and started for class together. Jennie, still exhilarated from the previous night, didn't notice at first how preoccupied Dean was as she babbled about one thing and another. In the face of his continued silence, however, she eventually picked up on his mood. She had been buoyant just a moment ago. Now she wasn't sure how she felt.

Something about the way Dean held himself back

worried her. Not in bed—there he was as eager as a starving man sitting down to his first meal in a month. He talked to her as he kissed and stroked her, and she loved that, loved hearing how much he wanted her and cherished her. But at other times he was so reticent, burying his feelings in silence. His conflict with his brother seemed a perfect example. Maybe, she reflected, that aspect of his personality was what allowed him to be the complete astronaut, shut in his space capsule, daring the elements to wrench a bead of sweat out of him. There he became Mr. Perfection, Mr. Cool.

She was still mulling this over when they went inside Building 10 and reached room 407, one of the classrooms that had become home for her over the past three years. Just like college, with its small blond Formica desk-and-chair sets and its blackboard flanking one wall. Who would ever know that many of the students who graced these cramped little rooms were professors themselves, paragons of erudition? NASA made no attempt to pander to the egos of its astronauts. If you had something to learn, even something as mundane as how to screw in a heat-shield tile while wearing gloves, you were supposed to learn it, period.

Jennie was always completely prepared for class. In the past few months, she'd literally had nothing to do except stay fit and study and work, and as a result, her research was moving along very quickly. She had given a variety of lectures to her classmates on the current status of weightlessness research, and she was fast becoming one of the noted authorities in America on the subject.

Academic achievement had always been easy for her; she felt confident with a textbook or a lecture. Yet, this morning, she remembered that there was a lot more to learning than what you could get out of a book or a lab test. Real life didn't come out of books, nor did passion. She wondered how much she really knew about anything—particularly about men.

As she took a seat beside Dean, she was aware of the concentration in her classmates' faces. Any one of them might get the mission; there was still one assignment to be made. Abigail Sarasin, for one, looked as if she would have jumped off the Empire State Building without a parachute if that would prove her worthiness. The first woman astronaut ever taken into the program, Abby was a legend among her colleagues. She was a geologist, a small woman capable of incredible intellectual feats. Her problem-solving abilities were extraordinary; everyone acknowledged this. And yet Abby, who had been Capcom three times, was a woman who was often called but never chosen. And there were others like her—competent and qualified but apparently not what the brass was looking for. Clearly, nobody had his or her mind on anything but the shoot.

Steve Akins watched the room fill up and then took his place in front of them at the podium. "Good morning, gentlemen—and ladies. I think last time we left off in the midst of a hot dispute on the motion disorientation question, so let's continue from there. Bob, you want to elucidate this for us?"

Dr. Robert Ricciardi had done some impressive work with isolation and disorientation over the past year. He'd also flown two missions and therefore had the experience in anti-gravity to call on in his research. So many of the astronauts got violently ill during their missions, suffering debilitating nausea and dizziness, that it was imperative for NASA to solve the problem quickly. What they did not want was a disabled astronaut, stuck outside the craft, trying to hoist, say, twelve hundred pounds of a TelStar satellite into the cargo bay and have him fall down on the job.

"Well, as we were saying," Bob began in his thick Brooklyn accent, "the crucial thing is to maintain the pilot's orthostatic ability and maintain strength for emergency egress from the craft, should that be necessary.

Okay, so you're sick—you feel so lousy you can't budge. We know it's not motion sickness, so drugs aren't the answer. The kind of reaction we get here on earth when we put a guy in the centrifuge chair for half an hour just isn't the same because of gravity. See, you don't *feel* as if you're upside down in space. Your eyes say you're floating upside down, but your inner ears say you're standing straight. The sick feeling is due more to neurological mixed signals—it's a psychological thing."

"Do you think jet lag is psychological?" asked Marty Hartsfield.

"Heck, no. Your body really does have those circadian rhythms to deal with. It knows when it's supposed to sleep and eat, and when you throw your schedule off, you get into trouble."

"But on earth, preflight adaptation is supposed to take care of that," Jennie cut in. "The whole theory probably goes to pot in space. Frankly, I'd suggest a radical alternative."

"What's that, Dr. Jacobs?" Steve Akins asked.

Jennie's eyes were twinkling. "I'd try sex."

Dean began coughing and couldn't stop. The four guys around him guffawed loudly.

"Did you say *sex?*" Akins jumped in, anxious that he not lose control of his class.

Dean shook his head. Jennie had done it again. You just didn't *say* things like that aloud in a NASA classroom. He decided to salvage the situation as best he could. "It could work," he put in, trying to make it sound as if they were discussing a particularly intricate engineering feat. "Look, we know that the adrenal secretions and the participation of the autonomic nervous system in complete relaxation do lessen the effects of jet lag on earth." He shrugged when he appeared to have convinced none of the hecklers. "Just an opinion."

"But I was serious." Jennie gave him a disparaging look. "They've proven it works when you're flying from

New York to London. Who knows what it would do out of our atmosphere?"

Rob Callahan grinned, twisting his thin mustache. "I can see the headlines now. 'G-Spots and Zero-G. Sex Found on Moon Voyage.' Don'tcha love it?"

The class was veering around the bend, and Steve, a man who lacked a sense of humor the way some people lacked tonsils, clearly didn't like it one bit. He attempted to regain some semblance of order. "I think we can move on to the disorientation segment of this. Jennie, what do you do on board to counteract these effects?"

"I don't think we've finished with the previous subject," Rob cut in. "Sex seems like something the government should get into—after properly researching it, of course. If I had someone to try it out with, I'd be happy to put together a manual for NASA." Rob glanced over at Darlene, who snorted loudly and glared at him.

Steve glanced anxiously at his watch and seemed relieved to realize that the hour was nearly over. "I'm letting you go early," he informed them. "Jennie, if you'd go over the isokinetic stuff for next time..."

"Yes, sir," she agreed, stifling a smile. As she gathered her papers and notebooks back into her attaché case, she couldn't help feeling rather pleased with herself.

But Dean burst her balloon. "What got into you in there?" he asked, steering her down the corridor.

"Oh, Dean, c'mon. I didn't say that to start a riot. I'd been doing some reading, and it really seemed like a possibil——"

"Jennie, you're a smart cookie, a damned good astronaut. The question is: Do you understand the rules of the game? I want you to win this one, but how are you going to do it if you can't play by their rules?" He looked at her intently. "See you later. Give it some thought."

She shook her head, remembering last night with Dean. He was so different with her here, at work. At one point— very late or very early, depending on your point of view— he'd pulled her over on her side and whispered that the next time he wanted to make her fly. And so they had. Together. But now he was all brass and polish, with no room for the least infraction. She wondered if he was right about her potential here, that she'd never win the game without playing by the rules. She certainly couldn't teach everyone else to play by hers.

She had ten minutes before her routine briefing, so she went to the small cubicle they called her office and dialed Florida directly.

There were some clicks and buzzes, and then Chris's phone began ringing. He picked up on the sixth ring. "What?" he demanded.

"Why so grouchy, ace?" Jennie smiled as she heard his voice. "If I were you, I'd go back to bed and try getting out on the other side."

"Hey, Jen! Great to hear your voice. Sorry to growl, but I'm having a tough morning, kid. I've been dragging this painting around the house, looking at it in different lighting, and it still stinks. What're you up to?"

"Thought I'd fly down this weekend to see you. How about it?"

"Hell, yes! Come *now*. Rescue me from this awful green wash."

Jennie laughed, imagining her paint-stained brother. Everything he did was gorgeous, every canvas sold for tons of money, and yet he claimed to hate it all. "I have a briefing, and being stuck in one of those is worse than being stuck in a vat of ochre. Expect me Saturday morning sometime. Oh, say, is it okay if I bring a guest?"

"Well, blow me down! You wouldn't mean a male guest, would you?"

"I sure would."

"Dear heart of mine! Oh, Jen, tell me you're in love," he pleaded.

She stopped a second to think about that one. "Not yet. But he's kind of wonderful. Another flyer," she warned Chris.

"You *are* a glutton for punishment—you know that?"

her brother said more seriously. "What am I going to do with you?"

"Just stand by me."

"You've got it. See you Saturday."

"Love to Molly and Timmy. Bye!"

She hung up, the smile refusing to leave her lips. Then she happened to look down at her watch.

"Oh, no! Late!" She ran down the corridor to her briefing, asking herself why she was perennially *not* on time to these dull sessions with the administrative types. She always had a problem keeping herself from dozing off at these meetings. There was nothing like an hour of NASA bull thrown by the very people who'd invented it.

She raced around to Building 4 and fairly catapulted herself down the corridor and into the briefing room. Naturally, everyone was waiting for her. Peter Reinhardt was there already, as was Colonel Andersen. Also present were two men from mission planning, two lawyers, and two people who invariably showed up at these events and never introduced themselves. Jennie thought they might be presidential advisors, but she wasn't sure. They nodded to her briefly but seemed to be very involved in their own discussion. She retreated to one end of the large mahogany table, praying that another astronaut would walk in soon. There was a certain amount of strength in numbers.

"Dr. Jacobs, we've asked the other people who were supposed to be present to come in a little later," Colonel Andersen began. "So we may as well get started. Peter?" He gave the floor to the man on his left.

"Dr. Jacobs," Peter Reinhardt began, "I have the pleasure of informing you that you are the final mission specialist to be chosen for the upcoming flight in two weeks."

Jennie tried to keep her mouth closed, but she simply couldn't. "You—you mean," she stammered, "I'm—

I'm really going?" She had an almost uncontrollable urge to jump out of her seat and turn a cartwheel, right there in front of everyone. "I'm honored, sir. Thank you for the vote of confidence," she added, quickly recovering. Jen, try not to grin like a high-school senior who's just been invited to the prom, for heaven's sake! she warned herself.

"We did have our reservations about you, Doctor, as I'm sure you're aware," Colonel Andersen cut in sternly. "You lack the proper preparation for parts of this mission."

"On the other hand," said one of the advisors, a tough-looking woman in a somber blue suit, "you have certain qualifications that we cannot overlook—particularly for the job we have in mind."

"And what is that?" Jennie asked hesitantly. Everyone in the room seemed terribly grim.

"Your psychological profile exactly matches our requirements for isolation in space," explained one of the men from mission planning. "We'd like you to try to tolerate three weeks. Naturally, Ann Lorge will be giving you round-the-clock training. Don't fail us, Doctor. There's a lot riding on this one."

"If there are no questions, the rest of us will convene now and let you get started. Your complete briefing should be ready by Tuesday. Thank you, Dr. Jacobs. You are dismissed," Colonel Andersen told her.

She sat there, stunned, stupefied, unable to let the reality penetrate. She was going up! And what was even stranger, she was going to be shut away, alone, in the silence of space.

"Needless to say, Jennie, what we tell you from here on in is strictly confidential. Aside from the fact that you're going up, not even the rest of your crew should know the nature of your assignment until we're ready to tell them."

She wanted to shout her joy to the world, but she

couldn't possibly have said a word to anyone. Her
mouth—and maybe her brain, as well—had just stopped
functioning.

- 7 -

SHE DIDN'T KNOW what to do first. Dean was in the shuttle module all morning, and it was out of the question to disturb him. Ann had other people programmed before her, so she couldn't simply barge in. Ann undoubtedly knew the good news anyway.

She went to her office and called her parents. The long-distance calls were strained sometimes, since neither Dr. John nor Dr. Beatrice Jacobs liked being interrupted at work, but this was top priority. Their patients would just have to take a breather.

Her father was dumbfounded, not quite able to grasp what she was saying. After about a dozen repetitions, Jennie threw up her hands, told him she had to get her mother on the phone, and that she'd drop him a note all about it. Then she hung up. She loved her father dearly, but he insisted on being stubbornly thick at the most crucial moments.

Upon hearing Jennie's news—and her orders to say nothing about the assignment to *anyone*—her mother was delighted but terrified. "What if something goes wrong— can you handle it?" was her first question. And her second query was, "Why do you have to be alone for three weeks?" The overly protective attitude was an integral part of her mother's makeup; she'd always had it, even about something as simple as Jennie's remembering her galoshes for a walk in the rain. It was true, she thought as she hung up: You may win the Nobel Prize, but you're always going to be your parents' little girl.

She had her hand on the receiver, wondering if she could get Susan out of the classroom at this hour, when the telephone rang. She jumped, then grabbed it. "Hello?"

"Jennie! I feel awful about not calling sooner. This case has had me really bollixed up. It's Jim Bradshaw," he added when she didn't say anything.

"Hi, how've you been?" She wondered what Dean would think if she said his brother had called her again. He'd probably fly off the proverbial handle.

"My patient's going into surgery tomorrow, and he's needed a lot of hand-holding. It's a good thing I came down with him, even though it's kept me from other things I'd rather be doing—like being with you, Jennie." His voice was light and flirtatious. "Well, what's new?" he asked jovially.

She laughed happily. "A lot, actually. I got assigned. I'm going up in two weeks. Same flight as your brother."

"Hey, that's tremendous! We have to celebrate. How about tonight? I'll pick you up at your place and—"

"Jim, I'm really sorry, but I can't. They're going to be prepping me around the clock for this. I'll have to be studying at night from now on to get acquainted with the craft and the payload. I have two weeks to learn everything; I can't tell you how terrified I am."

"C'mon, you have to have *some* time to yourself. And as a physician, I'm advising you not to skip meals. If I'm around, you won't be able to." He was cajoling now, clearly determined not to take no for an answer.

"Really, I'm booked. From racquetball to keep me in shape to intensive management of an anti-gravity toilet."

"When are you playing racquetball? You'll probably beat me badly, but my ego can take it. Please, Jennie. I'd really like to see you."

He was so persistent. She sighed, wondering whether she should give in. Probably the best thing to do was come right out and say everything at once, just the way she always did. If he took offense, that was his problem.

"Look, I know I don't really have to go into all this, but I want to tell you that your brother and I . . ." She stopped, not knowing what to say. *Your brother and I slept together? We're dating? We like each other a lot?* Everything sounded stupid and inconclusive. And as a scientist, there was nothing worse for Jennie than being purposely vague. "I just want to make it perfectly clear that this is only a racquetball game, nothing more," was what she finally came out with.

"Hey, don't you think I know that? I'm not dumb, Jennie. I just like being with you. And I'm glad you care about Dean—honestly. He needs someone like you—not that he deserves you. But as I told you, he's got the deep soul and I don't. I'm licked before I begin. But I'd still like to play ball. I need the exercise. What time's good for you?"

Later, when she thought about agreeing to meet him, she assumed she'd just been so excited that she had to share it with somebody. She figured Dean wouldn't be too pleased about it, but he seemed overly suspicious when it came to his brother. Maybe when she realized that friendship and exercise were the only things on Jim's mind, he'd get over it.

The craziness started as soon as she went over to Ann's office. Ann loaded her down with manuals on everything from the design of the shuttle to the electrical power system, the environmental controls, the module exchange mechanism, the guidance system, and the hygiene system. This was the fifth trip out for the *Liberator,* so naturally NASA was completely confident about it. Since everybody knew how this shuttle behaved, it wouldn't take much getting used to, even for first-time flyers. But there was something unusual about this mission that no one was discussing. In general, astronauts were assigned about a year in advance of a flight and went into training on the equipment seven to nine months prior to the launch. Here, on this rush job, there was scarcely enough time to figure out who would be doing what and for how long. Very curious. Jennie listened, took notes, then went to work.

"But I still want to know about this isolation thing," she said as she and Ann joined a group of other astronauts and several trainers in the experimental physical lab. "How do they keep me separate from the rest of the crew? And for what purpose? Isn't that going to mean separate facilities built into the craft?" As thrilled as she was, she couldn't get over the irony that up there in space, where she'd longed so to be, she would have to be parted from the man she had recently discovered she was crazy about. Three whole weeks. But that would be three weeks to make a splash—her own splash—in the world of aerospace flight. Which did she want more? If she weren't so all-fired competitive, she would have known the answer in a second.

"I can't tell you anything about the isolation," Ann declared brusquely. "And you should keep your mouth shut, too," she hissed.

"I know, I know. But I'm the one who's doing it. I have a right to be informed," she insisted. "Especially since I'm totally and completely petrified," she added in a whisper.

Ann's answer was to strap her into her centrifuge chair and tell everyone else to gather around and watch. A technician in a white lab coat rushed over and began attaching sensors to her arms, chest, and legs. "We're timing this one, Jennie," she informed her. "Hang on and breathe!"

Just as the device was activated, the door to the lab opened and Dean walked in. There was no way to unbuckle herself and run to him, so she just gave him a smile wide enough to part the Red Sea. He mouthed the words, "I've heard." Then she couldn't see anything else because she was spinning, slowly at first, at the end of a mechanical arm. It was like one of those carnival rides where the thing started up and your adrenaline pumped and you knew it was going to be unbearable in a second, but at the beginning it would be a lot of fun. Jennie, who knew what was coming, hung on for dear life.

She heard voices murmuring around her, trainers explaining various principles of velocity and acceleration, but she could only think about maintaining her center of balance. Everything she'd ever learned about the human body came into play now. Like a ballet dancer, she focused on the designated mark on the wall, whipping her head each time the chair brought her past it. If you didn't spot, you'd be dizzy within seconds.

The chair moved faster now, and the spectators were just a blur. A lot of people passed out when they spent too much time in this contraption; it was vital that Jennie show everyone how well tuned her body was.

It was starting to hurt. The pressure behind her eyes threatened to overwhelm her, but she kept breathing. There's nothing to this, she told herself calmly, though she knew her respiration and blood pressure, not to mention her pulse, were way up. She thought of the great yogis, able to control all their bodily functions. Well, kid, she mused, guess you don't qualify for perfection. She knew her sensors were charting really high figures, but there was nothing she could do about that. As long as she tolerated it, she passed.

There was no way to enjoy this exercise. In a brief ten minutes, Jennie was terribly disoriented. Time was meaningless in the centrifuge, and so was any coherent arrangement of your limbs. It was actually hard to tell

where your limbs were or what they were doing. When
you started to feel dizzy, you breathed more deeply, from
your diaphragm. And if you got panicky, you tried to
clear your mind of all thought. For Jennie, of course,
that was impossible. Dean was the first object of her
attention. A few minutes later, she started to replay the
delights of the previous night. Wasn't it odd? Here she'd
been celibate for two years and hardly ever thought about
it. But now that Dean had reawakened her, she was
hungry for more. She could remember their bodies, locked
together, rocking in sensual unity; she could remember
the words he spoke and the thoughts he only implied.
Mostly, she could remember the way she felt about him—
eager, longing, becoming more herself the more she was
with him.

The room was lost to her now. Her altered perception
made it impossible to determine where she was or how
fast she was whizzing around. The arm moved her faster,
and for a second she felt slightly sick to her stomach.
With another breath the nausea left her, and she kept
going easily for an additional fifteen minutes. She hardly
even realized it when the machine began slowing down
and she could see clear images of faces again. When the
thing finally stopped, she had been in rapid motion for
half an hour.

"Not too bad," Ann murmured, checking the various
screens that had charted Jennie's vital signs. "You'll need
some more of that, though. Next!"

Now came the real test. She had to get out of the chair
and walk—not stagger, not fall flat on her face—across
the room. Moving very carefully, she pinpointed Dean
several yards away and started toward him. Not too fast,
she thought. And don't smile; it wastes energy. With
fierce deliberation, she managed to get to him without
stumbling.

"Can't walk a straight line, eh? Next we give you the
breathilizer test, lady." He smiled, and then, right there

in front of everybody, he kissed her. If she hadn't been
dizzy before, she certainly was now. She was also turning
a deep shade of pink.

"I made it," she whispered, leaning against him. If
people were staring, she didn't care.

"I always knew they'd pick you."

"You did not. You told me just this morning I had a
lot to learn." She grinned but started weaving, and he
had to catch her and hold her steady.

"Sometimes I'm wrong. Sweetheart, I'm really happy
for you." He spoke close to her ear, his soft breath stirring
the red curls and making her heady with excitement.

"Dean, I don't know if I can do it," Jennie confessed
quietly. "What if I botch up the mission?"

"What if you stop worrying and get to work, huh?"
he asked her intently. "The great part is, we're going to
see those sunsets together." His voice was hypnotic,
soothing, and filled with promise. But when she leaned
away from him, she was surprised to see the glint gone
from his eyes. Once again, he looked completely hardnosed and professional.

"But—" Then she remembered: She wasn't supposed
to tell him about the isolation. "Listen, I got hold of my
brother. We're expected Saturday morning at Duck Key,
if you can get off."

"I already checked. All's clear." He looked at her with
those midnight blue eyes as though he couldn't wait to
get her alone. "Sounds like a great place. Ducky, in fact."

"Ooh." She grimaced. "I have the flight plans in my
desk drawer. We can look them over tonight—if tonight's
still okay," she added somewhat shyly.

"Okay? Are you kidding? It's all I've been thinking
about for hours."

"Jennie!" Ann called. "You're on duty, you know."

Jennie sighed. "An astronaut's day is never done.
Rescue ball is next."

"I'm on my way to a flight class. See you for dinner.

Did you say you were playing racquetball?"

"Yes." She decided to risk his wrath, feeling that being up front and open would allay any suspicions he might have. "Guess who I'm playing with."

"If I know you, it's probably King Kong. Anything for a bigger challenge. Meet you afterward, my car, about six."

"Dean—" she began, but it was too late. He was out of the room and running, and she still didn't have her balance back.

"Jennie, what are you waiting for?" Ann came up and took her by the arm. "We need you in here on the double."

Jennie looked back once, biting her lip. She should have made sure she told him. It was always easier to explain something before the fact than after. Reluctantly, she followed Ann to the next chamber of horrors.

"You know the routine on this one," Ann was saying. "Just let me get set up with the guys in the booth." She left Jennie standing in the middle of the isolation room, still pensive, still confused. It was so quiet in here, just as it might be in space. She walked around the room, lightly touching the walls. She'd made almost a complete circle when she noticed one of her fellow astronauts standing outside the door. It was Abby.

"I hear you've been assigned. Congratulations."

Jennie couldn't miss the pain behind Abigail's eyes, and she could feel it in her own gut. "It was just that my specialty was going to come in handy. You know."

This was totally ridiculous. She was apologizing for being selected.

Abigail just stared at her with large, luminous brown eyes.

"Abby," Jennie said softly, "I know how you must feel . . ."

"Of course you don't," the woman snapped in annoyance. "But don't let it bother you." She stalked off in a rage, leaving Jennie bruised and throbbing—and remembering her own similar response the time Dean had tried to console her. She knew it wasn't her fault that Abby still had no assignment—there were many others in the program who were in the same situation— but Jennie felt for them all. And it tarnished her own joy in her accomplishment.

"What got into her?" Ann asked, but she didn't wait for an answer. "Okay, get in the bag."

"I feel awful," Jennie murmured, following Ann to the equipment. "Like I stole something from her, something I can't give back."

"Hey, you." Ann stared at her grimly, an expression of concern creasing her brow. "Don't start feeling sorry for the others. If you do, you're lost. It's every man for himself here, and every woman, too. What you won, you won fair and square. For some reason, you're the most desirable candidate for this shoot. No telling when Abigail will be needed just as badly as you're needed now."

But as Jennie climbed inside the rescue ball, a kind of bowling bag just big enough for one person to squeeze into, she couldn't help herself. It was hard for her to reconcile her good luck with someone else's misfortune.

She had just gotten herself settled when Ann came rushing back into the room and unzipped her. "Good news!" Ann smiled. "You don't need to work on this one." She handed her a hastily handwritten memo from Peter Reinhardt. "They want you in a suit."

"But that means . . ." Jennie looked at the memo, extremely puzzled.

"You're getting launched away from the main craft. When they say isolation, they *mean* it."

Ann left her with a schedule of appointments, tests, and briefings for the next day, then told her to get some rest. As Jennie wandered out of the lab, she didn't feel quite as confident as she had previously. It was one thing to be shut in a little cubicle away from Dean and the rest of the crew; it was quite another situation to be making your own orbit, all by yourself, in the midst of a hundred million stars.

There was no one in the locker room except Darlene, who was getting ready for her daily weight-training workout. With muscles so highly developed, she had to keep them constantly in shape. The guys were always asking if they could feel her biceps, and she was forever Indian-wrestling them to the ground. The funny thing about her was that when she left work, it was to go home to her lawyer-husband and her two-year-old twins—not exactly the image of the fearless, powerful space traveler.

"Hail, the conquering hero!" Darlene exclaimed. She pumped Jennie's hand for a minute, then let her go and embraced her in a big bear hug.

"Well, I don't feel much like a hero." Jennie grinned, massaging her arm. She wished Darlene would learn that her unabashed enthusiasm was sometimes awfully painful to others. "I feel totally ill-prepared. Two weeks to learn everything!"

"You'll do it, babe. I have no doubt. What's your assignment?"

Jennie tugged her T-shirt off over her head. "Top secret. Even I don't know."

"Oh, come *on.*"

"I'm serious." Jennie stripped down to her daring underwear, then replaced it with her serious workout set. Over her practical jogging bra and pants, she donned a short side-split white skirt and a pink singlet with mesh inserts. She ran a comb through her auburn curls and hastily put a headband over them. "Can't talk about it now, Darlene." Or probably ever, she told herself as she raced to the front appointment desk. Jim was leaning over it, cradling the telephone between his ear and shoulder.

It was impossible not to compare the two brothers

physically. Dean's body was all hard rock, muscle piled on muscle, making him seem massive and even taller than his six feet. Jim, on the other hand, was rangy, with thin legs and a slimmer torso.

His eyes lit up when he saw her, and a smile curved the corners of his wide mouth—the only feature he had in common with Dean.

He stood up straighter. "Got to sign off now, sweets," he said into the receiver. "Keep that in mind—what I mentioned, okay? See you." As he rested the receiver in its cradle, he stared pensively at Jennie, a look of wonder on his face.

"Has anyone ever told you that you're lovely when you play racquetball?" he whispered so that the people milling around the area couldn't hear.

She smiled at the compliment. The guy was incorrigible! "No, just sweaty. You ready to get beat bad, mister?"

"I suppose," he sighed.

She checked in with the attendant and signed for their court, then led him down the long cement-block corridor to the tiny door with only a slim panel of glass at the top to spy into.

"Volley for serve?" she asked him.

"That's okay. You start out. I'll watch you."

She shrugged and walked to the server's box in the center of the court, then slammed a hard one off the far wall. It ricocheted against a side wall before bouncing on the floor. Jim lunged for it and passed it back to her, but she was too quick for him. She swiveled her body as she swung her racket, causing the ball to change course and hit the back wall first. It was an impossible return. Jim missed.

"Whew! Pretty competitive, aren't you?" he said teasingly as he panted.

"I play hard," she admitted. "Score is one–zero. You ready for the next?" She *was* competitive—there was no denying it. Regardless of how guilty she might feel about

Abigail, she had wanted that job more than anything in the world. Winning did something for her, and it was evident that this man beside her wasn't really crazy about that. His brother, on the other hand, would have been cheering her on, daring her to beat him.

She worked at the game, not deliberately trying to cream Jim, but succeeding easily in foiling him with her careful strategy. Racquetball wasn't a lot of fun unless you were good enough to place your shots, and Jennie outclassed her opponent in this. When the score was fifteen to ten, her favor, he begged for a halt.

"I'm out of condition, I admit. Can we just volley a little?"

"Sure. Forget the game."

"Lord, how can I? I used to be a cham-peen athlete, you know. Now, here I am, reduced to incipient middle age, with a lady astronaut beating me rotten."

"Oh, and is that such a come-down?" she asked, indignant. "I happen to be one of the best around here. You should count yourself fortunate to have such a tough opponent."

He shook his head. "Really. Well, I suppose I'm doomed to sit on the sidelines, watching others better than myself climb to the top."

"Aw, poor dear," she clucked, relenting.

"Well, speaking of me on the sidelines, tell me, now that I can breathe a little, how *are* things going with my brother? I mean, there's really not a prayer for me? I can't change your mind?"

She laughed at his hopeful enthusiasm. Jim reminded her of a big friendly dog, one who would never stop trying too hard to please.

"You're really in love with Dean, then?"

"I . . . I don't know. I guess I'm . . . I really can't talk about it now. Tune in next month." She was always embarrassed about discussing her private feelings with anyone, let alone with the brother of the man she so passionately wanted in her life.

"The time's about up, thank goodness," Jim said, picking up the can of balls. "I couldn't hit another. But thanks for giving me a workout." She was glad he wasn't going to press her to confide in him. "Shall we?" He put his weight against the heavy door to the court and pushed outward, letting her duck under his arm. She was smiling back at him when she realized someone was waiting on the other side.

It was Dean. "I got through early, so I thought I'd—" His words broke off as he saw Jim right behind her. Suddenly, he was the embodiment of rage, his body a steel rod, ready to do damage. "What the hell!"

"Dean, wait a minute," Jennie began. But he didn't give her a chance.

"I warned you once, Jennie. And that does it." He turned on his heel and propelled himself down the corridor, wanting more than anything to get away from the scene he'd just stumbled upon.

- 8 -

DEAN DROVE LIKE a madman away from the center, anger clicking through him like a train running wild down a track. If he'd been a different make of man, he might have cried, but he couldn't remember the last time he'd done that.

It was rotten luck, that was all. He thought he had something special going with Jennie, this soft woman who touched him where he'd never felt anything but dull complacence before. But if she really was as crazy about him as he was about her, then what in God's name was she doing with his brother?

When he reached the turnoff for Tuscaloosa, he kept going straight, right to the bay. There was a small cove nearby, a place he sometimes went to think. On this warm August evening, there was nothing he needed more.

The path was deserted, as it always was. He pulled himself out of the Stingray and locked it, brushing back the lock of dark blond hair that had fallen into his face.

That brother of his! He'd always trusted him, except for that once. He wanted to trust him now, and yet . . . Long ago, he'd relegated the incident with Marilyn to oblivion, deciding that it really was all her fault, that his brother was a flirt, sure, but not deliberately manipulative or evil. Actually, Jim had probably done him a big favor. He'd been lying to himself, lying about love, about his life, about what he really wanted in a woman. The only thing he knew was jets, and that didn't wash with Marilyn. She was all set for a house in the suburbs and a station wagon filled with two-point-five kids and a collie. Dean knew he wasn't ready for that. And maybe his ambivalence showed. Jim, on the other hand, didn't have an ambivalent bone in his body. When he arrived on the doorstep that Christmas Day, all shiny and new from medical school in Canada, he was irresistible. Any woman would have gone for him. Right?

"Hell!" Dean kicked a spray of gravel, wondering for the first time in ten years whether he'd been wrong. Was it possible? His own brother, for heaven's sake? Could he have really plucked that woman right from under his nose? And was he about to do it again?

And what was he supposed to think about Jennie? That crazy woman! Sometimes she reminded him of a whole field of butterflies after a spring rain, free but easily captured, and sometimes she was just like that hummingbird he'd described, too fast to catch.

Maybe he was jealous because she *was* so exceptional, and maybe there was nothing to worry about. A dinner and a racquetball game? What could it mean? Maybe there was a perfectly logical explanation for her seeing Jim again. Maybe it was all as innocent as could be . . . maybe.

Talking—that was what she'd probably prescribe. He got the distinct impression she was a big one for talking. Dean found it hard to string two words together when he was riled up. All he wanted to do was kick these stones clear to kingdom come.

Not too enlightened, mister, he told himself in a moment of lucidity. He started back for the car just as the sliver of a moon made its appearance in the dusky sky. You sound like a real jerk. Why don't you think the whole thing over before you ditch this relationship?

He'd waited years for a woman like Jennie. If he lost her, it might just be *the* mistake of his life.

"Well, he sounds like a perfect lunatic!" Susan exclaimed. Jennie was sitting in her kitchen, drinking massive quantities of apple juice. "Hey, go easy on that stuff. God knows what it does to your kidneys," Susan joked when her miserable friend poured herself a fifth glass.

"I'm addicted to it," Jennie murmured. "Let me drown my sorrows, please."

"All right, look at it this way, baby." Susan sat beside her, flung her golden mane over one shoulder, and took Jennie's hand. "The relationship hadn't gone very far. One night of rapture is just that—one night. Not that you don't deserve more—you certainly do—but at least you didn't get yourself all hung up on him."

"But that's the problem. I *am* hung up on him already. Did you ever have a feeling that everything clicked with a person? That you could just reach out and touch his mind and his emotions?"

Susan wrinkled her nose. "What do his emotions feel like?"

"Be serious, will you?" Jennie was exasperated. Even her best friend couldn't understand this. "I'd hardly looked at a man since Andy, and now I feel as if that marriage is a thing of the past. Finally I can let go of the person I was and move on."

"Who were you?" Susan asked quizzically. They'd only really become good friends in the past year.

"Well, for one thing, I was harder."

"What?"

"Does that sound strange? I had this shell on, and things didn't really penetrate it. Andy and I were great pals, and we allowed each other all the freedom we needed. It was a really loose marriage—we even lived in different places for most of it. What woman would put up with that? But I did; I just went with the flow. Andy wanted to work till he dropped, so I did the same. I didn't allow myself any feelings.

"But now I do, Susan, and this man is woven into all of them. It's not that I'm a totally new person, you see. It's not that I've stopped pushing for the top, but it's with a different kind of momentum. I've made time for being me. And I think what I want more than anything is real closeness. The other night, I thought I'd found it." She sighed and took her juice to the window, looking out at the late afternoon sun tingeing the bay with hazy light.

She turned back to her friend with something like envy in her hazel eyes. "You have a baby on the way; you have a guy you'd lie down and die for—"

"Well, I wouldn't go *that* far," Susan interrupted.

"But I only have the beginnings of what I want. And I keep thinking that if I hadn't agreed to the stupid racquetball game, I'd be on the road to getting it all."

"Sweetheart, you're blaming yourself for nothing. You've had an incredible day, after all—assigned to the shoot, a devastatingly wonderful astronaut eaten up with jealousy over you—why, it's like something out of a novel!"

"Yeah, a science fiction novel," Jennie quipped.

"I bet Dean'll forgive and forget. You go see your relatives this weekend, and let him stew for a bit. Sometimes men need to be kept hanging," Susan said, acting for all the world like the experienced and knowledgeable femme fatale. Jennie suspected that, in reality, she was just as naïve about relationships with men as Jennie was.

Jennie grunted and took the last slug of her juice before getting up and going to the door. "I'm the one hanging, though. And Dean's not the forgiving-and-forgetting type. He seems to have a grudge against his brother that goes back years. I'm not sure I haven't just been added to the list of atrocities between them." She grabbed her briefcase and put her hand on the doorknob. "Thanks for listening, pal."

"Anytime. And say," Susan called when her friend was halfway down the driveway, "congratulations! This is one time I'll be glued to the TV for all the coverage."

Jennie smiled wanly and wandered across the yard, hopping over the privet hedge into her own territory. The talk had been cathartic, but she still felt lousy. She was also floating in apple juice.

She had just raced Wings into the bathroom when she heard a car in the driveway. She felt her heart beating rapidly, and as she ran to the door, she could almost *see* him standing on the other side. She flung it open, her face glowing.

"I'm terribly sorry to disturb you at home, Jennie. I wouldn't but . . . extreme circumstances require extreme measures."

Jennie felt everything inside her cave in. It was Peter Reinhardt. "It's perfectly all right. Won't you come in?"

He followed her inside. He looked weary, and older than his fifty-odd years. His tie was askew, and even the helmet of silver hair looked a little out of place.

"Can I offer you a drink?" she asked hesitantly, unsure of the protocol in this situation. She was dying to know why he had come to her home, but it was in the nature of the "right-stuff" mentality that you weren't supposed to ask questions like that. Jennie had always been the one in the program to blurt out everything that came into her head, but she held her tongue for once.

"I'd love some Scotch, if you have it. Just one cube."

"Coming up." She padded into the kitchen and poured Peter a stiff drink. She considered the condition of her kidneys, then shrugged and got herself a glass of white wine. When she joined him in the living room a few minutes later, Wings was already seated comfortably in his lap.

"Cats. Great companions, aren't they?" Peter smiled a little, stroking the thick black-and-orange fur. "You could probably do a lot worse than to have this little fella up in the module with you. Thanks," he added, taking the drink she offered and downing a third of it in one gulp.

"I wouldn't mind having her along," Jennie acknowledged. She was getting impatient now. If he didn't say something soon, she was going to give in to her desperate need to ask a battery of questions.

"Jennie, I'll be honest. I guess you know this isn't merely a social call. It's about office business. I just couldn't bring myself to tackle it at the center. All these years in service, all my experience, and I have to admit, sometimes my assignments are still beyond me."

Jennie mentally sat on her hands. She was slowly going out of her mind.

"Basically, why I'm here is . . ." He cleared his throat, drank again from his glass. "I have to grill you a little, see what's going on with you. I'm not a psychologist, and supposedly they've got plenty of guys on staff who could do this, but they've put it to me, since I know you pretty well. So you're stuck with me."

Jennie sat there, biting her tongue. If she bit it any harder, it was going to fall off.

"It's about this shoot. I guess you've figured that something was up, since NASA doesn't generally schedule missions this precipitously—and it certainly doesn't select its crews with only two weeks' notice."

"I was curious about that, as a matter of fact." Curious! Ha! What an understatement!

"Well, the scientific work we've been doing in space is just a preliminary. That is, someone's going to have to stay up there for a while and work on long-term projects, and we want to make sure that sensory or emotional deprivation isn't going to impede our progress. They're worried as hell about the Russians staying up for almost a year—well, you know that."

"Yes. Peter, I don't mean to be rude, but . . ." Maybe another drink would loosen him up? She suddenly saw herself sitting across from him as if she were floating above the scene. There was Jennie with a big cartoon bubble over her head, a large question mark growing inside. Pretty soon, the thing would explode, and Peter Reinhardt would have half of her living room splattered all over him.

"No, no. Not rude at all. It's understandable that you'd be nervous." He looked into his empty glass, and she took the hint. This time, she brought the Scotch bottle to him.

"That's awfully good of you." He poured, then held the drink. He was very quiet for a few minutes. It was the last straw.

"Peter, what is it, for heaven's sake! What could be so awful that you can't tell me?" She knew she had broken the cardinal rule, but there was nothing she could do. The words were out of her mouth.

"Yes, well, certainly." He harrumphed and stared straight at her. "Here goes. We're putting you up there for three weeks in your own module—I guess you've discovered that much already. As far as the American public will know, you're going to be alone, in separate orbit, carrying out some weightlessness experiments. In reality, however, you'll have someone with you. We've decided that you and Dean Bradshaw will make for the most dynamic interaction. His psychological tests and yours match up in the most fascinating ways. Fascinating!"

Jennie looked down at her shoes, then blinked a couple of times. In her wildest dreams, she had, of course, pictured herself and Dean happily ensconced in a little module, cast away on a desert island in space. Now the picture didn't seem quite so idyllic.

"You and Dean do . . . uh . . . get along, am I correct?" Peter asked gently.

"Well, we . . . yes, we do, but—" That was not exactly a lie. Not exactly.

"And you would not be averse to spending three weeks together alone? We hesitate to disclose this kind of mission to the American public, you see. A lot of folks out there would strenuously disapprove of an unmarried man and woman orbiting the earth together for three weeks. And with the various problems NASA has been having lately, we can't risk any bad publicity."

"I understand. But, Peter—"

"So when we broadcast shots of the crew on board the main shuttle, we'll make sure to flash some of the initial ones we'll take of Dean on the first day. Ah, the wonders of the camera's tricks. I love it when we beat the media at their own game." He chuckled.

"It sounds like a difficult—"

"Now, you should know that once inside the module, you're not going to have the same opportunity for contact with ground personnel as the rest of the shuttle crew will. We *really* want you two to get that . . . uh . . . stranded feeling." He laughed jovially. "Not that you can't communicate if you have to, but we're going to leave the TV and radio hookups up to you both, at your discretion. We expect you to take thorough career activity plans aboard and carry them out. Also, we'll expect a moment-by-moment account of the mission in your debriefing sessions."

"Well, that's no problem, sir. But I just wonder about—"

"I'm certainly glad that's all settled, then." He downed the rest of his drink and got up abruptly, causing Wings to protest loudly. "And I thought all these personal questions were going to embarrass us both. Ha! Guess I could go into the shrink business after all, what do you say?" He grinned widely, obviously very pleased with himself. Jennie wasn't heartless enough to point out to him that he hadn't let her answer one single personal question.

Probably terrified of what would come out, she thought as she saw him to the door.

"Young lady, I'm very proud of you," Peter said, taking her hand and shaking it hard. "You're going to be another first in NASA history."

"I'm pleased to have been tried and found worthy, sir," she quipped.

The irony sailed right past him. "I know there's nobody else in the program who could do this. Oh, Darlene's a hard worker and Abigail's smart as a whip and Ann Ellen seems to be a crackerjack in emergencies, but there's no other woman like you."

Jenny looked at him quizzically. "Why? What have I got that they don't?"

"Well..." He fumbled for a second, then recovered. "You're an innovator. You're flexible. And frankly, you're the only one in the program wacky enough to try this." He chuckled again. "I meant that as a compliment—really I did, Jennie."

"I know. I took it as one." She was biting her cheeks to keep a straight face. That was a new one—wacky! Except for her complicated love affair—not in the rule book—she felt she was making great progress in NASA terms, watching what she said and getting more conservative every day. Not to Peter's way of thinking, evidently.

"Good night, then. See you tomorrow. And I want you to take it easy this weekend. Go somewhere, do something... something..."

"Wacky?" she volunteered.

"That's it. Absolutely." He stalked off into the gathering dark, and she stood watching him, an indulgent smile lighting her face.

Now, why was he so panicked about keeping this a secret? Or was the government breathing down his neck? It seemed perfectly straightforward to her that two competent astronauts should be launched into space alone.

Unless they all thought . . . unless they simply assumed that a man and a woman alone couldn't keep their hands off each other. "More's the pity," she muttered as she walked back inside.

No, it was just the propriety of the thing. Two men alone—now that was teamwork. Two women alone was . . . let's see, they'd probably consider it a tea party. But a man and a woman—horrors!

As she picked up the glasses and carried them into the kitchen, it occured to her that she had a big problem— a very big problem. How was she ever going to manage three weeks alone with Dean after what had happened? It would be sheer agony to be locked up with someone who didn't want to see your face, particularly when that was the same someone who caused sparks to go off inside you every time you looked at him. She was dying to make it up with him, discuss the myriad feelings that had gotten hurt. But she wasn't going to go crawling to him. As far as she was concerned, she'd done nothing wrong. Still, he wasn't big on talking. What would they do up there for three weeks, for heaven's sake? Any way she looked at it, it was likely to be wonderful and terrible, both.

She checked out an old T-33 and cleared her flight with the ground controllers. It was a lovely day for flying—clear, no wind, only a few cumulus clouds in sight. As she took off, soaring above the flat Texas land-scape, she found that she was enormously happy to be leaving the Center for a few days. Seeing the same people, working at the same frantic pace—it was a perfect recipe for burnout, an illness she couldn't risk catching right now.

She'd dressed for the occasion, too. Instead of her daily army-drab wardrobe, she'd packed only bright and cheery clothes: a daring lavender-and-white tie-dyed silk blouse and tight sarong skirt for evening—which Chris would scoff at and Molly would love—and wild print clothes for daytime wear. This morning she had taken out her yellow-and-red Hawaiian shirt and the khaki pants that showed off her slim figure to best advantage. She felt like a bird unfettered, or maybe Amelia Earhart, as she zoomed off into the skies by herself that morning.

Chris, Molly, and Timmy were waiting for her at the tiny airstrip, Timmy proudly riding his father's shoulders as he waved at each small plane that came in for a landing. Jennie smiled as she taxied to a stop and waited for the ground crew to come and check her in. She never had enough time to spend with her terrific family; she was always catching them on the run.

"Ooh, Aunt Jennie, I saw you in the sky!" Timmy, a carrot-red-haired wonder with one blue eye and one brown, couldn't hug Jennie hard enough.

"Jen, how are you?" Molly asked, wresting her sister-in-law out of Timmy's death-grip embrace.

"Hi, sis." Chris, looking a little tired and harried, stroked his reddish-blond beard and grinned at her.

"Hi, ace." She hugged him, then leaned back to take them all in at a glance. "You must have been waiting here for hours."

"Timmy insisted. We got here about nine and have been checking in planes since then. I counted nineteen," Molly said.

"Which makes nineteen cups of coffee." Chris grimaced. "Say, where's your . . . ?" He looked around meaningfully.

"Unavoidable cancellation," Jennie said noncommittally. She picked up her duffel and led the way off the strip, pocketing the keys to the plane. "Seeing you for a whole weekend seems too good to be true."

"Yeah, well, it's not bad seeing you, either." Chris took her bag as they walked toward the stand of palm trees that swayed in the hot Florida breeze. "Say, what's all this Dad was trying to tell us on the phone the other night? Are you really going up?"

"You got it!" Jennie let Timmy take her hand and drag her toward the car. "I'm a full-fledged astronaut now," she told her nephew.

"Are you going to the moon?" he asked, wide-eyed.

"Well, not this week. But I might later on."

"Wow! Wait'll I tell Gus and Tony!"

Jennie thought there was nothing like the admiration in a seven-year-old's eyes. She'd seen something like that starry-eyed look on Dean's face in bed that night. Maybe it was something little boys never outgrew, but something grown men were afraid of revealing.

Why can't I stop thinking about him? she mused as she climbed into Chris's van and they drove away toward the shoreline. About his hands on me, his mouth covering mine. The way our bodies fit like pieces of a jigsaw puzzle. Oh, Jennie, stop it! she anguished. You're supposed to be having fun, she commanded herself harshly.

After a ten-minute drive along the coast, she could see the houseboat. Chris had painstakingly renovated an old tug, and it still bore traces of its former working life on the Keys. When he'd met Molly, he was still struggling to install a new boiler, and their tales of plumbing disasters never failed to send Jennie into stitches. Luckily, Molly was the kind of woman who rolled with the punches. Nothing seemed to perturb her—not even a lake in the middle of her bedroom.

"This is your weekend, kid, so you pick the activity schedule," Chris said as he parked her things in the little cubbyhole off the lower deck that was laughingly called a guest room.

"But I want to show Aunt Jennie my cove and the turtles and go to the aquarium and have a picnic in the rowboat," Timmy complained.

"There seems to have been a slight rearrangement in scheduling," Jennie told Chris before starting to tickle her nephew unmercifully. He submitted for only a second, then struggled free and took off after her, intent on revenge.

"Hey, monster!" Chris grabbed him around the waist and swung him out of the hatch. "What say we give your aunt a minute—no more—to clean up. Then we can sit and talk for a while."

"Talk? Yuk!" was Timmy's response.

Molly ducked her head in and handed Jennie a steaming cup of coffee. She was a tall brunette with pitch-black hair that hung in straight lines down her back like a comfortable shawl. Molly might not be a beauty, but she positively shone with accomplishment. Ten years ago, she'd been a major executive at a big Florida bank, pulling down a substantial salary. But when she met Chris, something had happened. She chucked the job and went to work with him on the houseboat, using her savings to pay people to do things Chris clearly wasn't capable of. Theirs was a truly symbiotic marriage; they nourished each other and cared for each other twenty-four hours a day. Which was no mean trick when Chris was late with a commission and acted like the world's worst jerk.

"You two guys get lost for awhile. I want to chat with this person. Women stuff!" Molly added when neither her husband nor son seemed inclined to leave. Slowly, they shuffled down the deck, leaving the two women alone.

"Jen, it's so neat to have this time with you. Boy, are you thin and gorgeous! How do you do it?"

"I just forget to eat." Jennie shrugged. She and Molly sat on the narrow bed together, feeling the boat rock under them.

"So, tell me about the gentleman," Molly insisted. "You note I don't even ask about your shoot first. Personal life is more important."

Jennie looked somber for a second, and Molly said, "I think I just put my foot in it."

"No, let's just say I thought it was something, and then it wasn't. I don't know if it's me or him—or destiny."

"Hey, I hate to interrupt." Chris stuck his head in the doorway again. "But we've got a visitor. Or, should I say"—he smirked at his sister—*"you've* got a visitor."

Another head appeared in the doorway, and Jennie's brain went whirling. She was hot and cold all at once, and her breath started coming in short gasps. For a second, she thought it must be an optical illusion—this massive masculine presence blocking the sunlight, looking as though it were completely natural and normal for him to be in Florida, on her brother's houseboat, grinning as if he'd just pulled the best practical joke in the world.

It was no illusion. Dean Bradshaw was there, and he'd come for Jennie.

- 9 -

"YOU LEFT THE flight plans in your drawer," he reminded her.

"Oh," she said stupidly, wanting to rush up and embrace him, wanting to ask if everything was all right again, but incapable of moving any muscles at all. She had no speech, no breath, nothing but the thought of him flooding over her.

"I didn't want to leave things the way they were," he explained softly. "And it couldn't wait till Monday." Still, he hadn't moved from the doorway.

"Well, I think I'll rustle up some lunch for us all," said Molly hastily. "It may take a while," she added with a laugh in her voice. "As a matter of fact, Chris and Timmy and I might have to run into town. Chris!" She beat a quick retreat under Dean's arm and out the hatch.

Dean cleared his throat, then took a step toward Jennie. "Well, are you glad to see me?" He felt dumb, even though he'd been pleased with himself for pulling this off. Maybe she wouldn't like it after all, he worried, looking into her frozen face. Even her flecked hazel eyes, always in motion, always seeking out something new, seemed glazed and fixed.

"Glad? I don't think that's the word," she whispered, finally finding her voice again.

The soft bed she was sitting on was inviting, but he didn't dare join her there. He simply couldn't tell what was going on between them. Better ask, he decided, steeling himself for the worst. "You're mad, right? You think I overreacted."

She sighed and looked at the floor for a moment. The swaying boat did nothing to calm her anxious stomach. "I *was* angry, yes—because I thought you didn't trust me." She looked at him keenly. "Do you?"

"I think I trust you more than I do myself."

She pursed her lips, frustrated with his apparent inability to say what he meant *when* he meant it. "All you had to do was ask," she chided. "Jim said he'd like to play racquetball; I said fine. End of story. Isn't that cut-and-dried enough for you? I had no legitimate excuse to turn him down."

"But why, after I told you about him?"

"Because!" she exploded. "Because what you told me about him happened once and never again. Because he seems like a perfectly nice guy, period. I think I'm a pretty good judge of human nature. I have to form my own opinions. I won't take someone else's and assume they're right. Even yours," she added emphatically. "Give me credit for the common sense I was born with, Dean."

He licked his lips and looked at the floor. "I know you're right—in here." He pointed to his head. "But it's here where I feel I shouldn't let go of my wariness." He put a hand over his heart.

"If you want me, if you think we can mean something to each other, you'll have to let go. Otherwise, it's probably better for me to butt out." *Say you don't want me out,* she begged him silently. *Say you never want me out.*

And suddenly, sitting there on that rocking boat, she

realized that she was in love, that she had fallen in love with this tough, tender, reticent astronaut who would pick himself up on a moment's notice and fly twelve hundred miles to see a woman he'd just been horribly upset with. The thought made her dizzy, and the wake of the sea made it worse. She hadn't eaten breakfast, either.

"I . . . oh, excuse me!" She bolted off the bed and out the door, down the narrow corridor to the head. Slamming the door behind her, she threw herself down on her knees over the bowl, as embarrassed as she'd ever been.

"Jennie, let me in! Let me help you, for heaven's sake!" he yelled, banging on the door.

"What's the matter?" Chris wandered down from the main deck, clearly convinced that another lovers' quarrel was in progress—and in his house. "Mister, that's my sister you're making miserable. I hope you know that."

"Chris!" Molly called from the minuscule kitchen in the back. "Leave them alone, will you?"

Timmy appeared around a bend. "Hey, what's happening?"

"You get lost!" commanded his father, rubbing his red beard with fury. "Now, I want to know what's going on!"

Before Dean had a chance to respond, the door to the head opened and Jennie walked out, looking pale and shaken. Chris put his arm around her protectively. "Sweetheart, what's this turkey been up to?"

Jennie started laughing, and then the laughter turned to tears. She didn't know whether she was hysterical or just wacky, as Peter Reinhardt had put it. "This turkey is a wonderful person, Chris. It's me who's the candidate for the loony bin." She smiled at Dean through her tears and reached for his hand. It was hard and calloused and warm, and the very touch of it steadied her anxious heart. "Did you ever feel so happy you got sick to your stomach?" she asked the two men.

Dean lifted one eyebrow in skeptical amusement. "Never," he told her.

"Not me. Whew! I thought for a second there was something fishy going on." Chris shook his head and lumbered back toward the stairs. "Okay, let's keep it as calm as possible now. Clear sailing and all that. Molly tells me that my family and I are going out for an hour or so. Hope you don't mind." He disappeared limb by limb up toward the main deck, leaving Dean and Jennie staring at each other.

"I'm sorry." Dean put out his arms, and she came to him.

"Sorry? What for? *I'm* the one causing the ruckus." She buried her face in his open khaki shirt, inhaling the clean smell of him, feeling the soft chest hairs run along her cheek like waving grass.

He lowered his head to her rumpled red-brown curls and nuzzled first one ear, then the other. "I didn't allow for any bad stuff coming between us. I wanted it all storybook-perfect from day one—no fuss, no muss. I guess in real life it's not like that. I had some growing up to do, Jennie. I still do."

"You and me both, cowboy." Slowly, their bodies hugging close, they made their way down the corridor back to her little cubbyhole. Jennie closed the door and threw the deadbolt.

"Ever made love on a boat?" she asked mischievously, already unbuttoning her blouse.

"I'm green," he admitted. "Will you show me how?"

"Let's show each other," she said, throwing off the blouse and letting it fall behind her. Her pants followed quickly after, and then her underwear—the plain beige non-sexy kind she usually wore.

He had never seen a body like hers. It was petite but strong, the pert breasts standing at attention like divers about to plunge off a high promontory into the sea. Her flat stomach tapered down to slender legs that had the power of steel springs. The color of her skin, pale and rosy, would have been impossible to capture on canvas;

no color on an artist's palette could match it. Seeing her there, offering herself to him so simply, so purely, he felt greedy and satiated at the same time. He wanted to crush her to him, but almost more than that, he wanted to continue absorbing the sight that made him ache with passion.

"Oh, Jennie, how I've missed you. I've wanted you in my bed, in my arms, every night." He raised his arms, and she walked into them, relishing the feel of his embrace. His mouth teased one excited nipple to a nearly intolerable state, and she moaned with pleasure, urging him on, speaking words she had never said aloud.

Her hands were busy now, fumbling with buttons and snaps, discarding one piece of his clothing after another. And when he was finally naked, he pulled her over on top of him on the tiny bunk, and they kissed deeply and fully, their tongues and teeth eagerly seeking out unexplored areas. She felt him bite her lower lip, and the mood took her.

"Wanna play rough, huh?" she asked teasingly. She countered with a soft bite to his golden-haired chest, and then she was all over him, her body flailing and thrashing as she worked him into a frenzied ecstasy equal to her own. The two of them were lost in a sea of hot energy, the currents passing from one to the other.

When he reached down to caress her intimately, he thrilled to her dusky moisture. She held him close to her, rubbing her skin against his, cherishing the very distance that separated them because it meant they could go still further together. And when they finally joined their bodies, it was with a furious rush of speed, a demanding and pulsing rhythm that encouraged a turbulent end to their delicious labor.

"Wait just a second," he panted, steadying himself on her shoulders. "Lie still for a minute."

And so she lay against him, feeling nothing but the throb of his blood in hers, the huge fullness inside her.

She gripped him hard, then released him, then gripped him again. He closed his eyes, biting his lip hard to restrain himself. "Jennie," he said, "you'll be the death of me."

"Don't be silly," she told him tenderly. "There's so much life there I can't contain it all."

And then, with a smile, he rolled her over onto her back and began to move again, slowly at first, then increasing his pace until they were both sweating and ready. He saw her face contort with delight and anguish, and she was making sounds that came from deep within her, sounds she probably couldn't even hear because she was too involved with him and his pleasure. She cried out over and over, her head falling back in total ecstasy. And then he was with her, his own joy matching hers completely, and they were united with a bond unequal to any other.

Afterward, they were still and silent, gazing into each other's eyes, existing on the rapture that shone back and forth between them. The soft rocking of the boat soothed them now, and they went with its gentle ebb and flow.

"It's all right to get mad at someone you care about," she said, "as long as you know how to make up."

"You know, you're right. I have a problem about getting mad. I don't think I ever really let myself let go before this. I figured it would ruin everything." He looked slightly abashed.

"It only makes for more things to share, really." She thought ruefully that she was no expert on the matter. She and Andy had fought all the time but hadn't had a clue as to how to fight constructively. It all seemed so long ago now, in that time when she was someone else. Someone who didn't know Dean Bradshaw.

"As long as we're in the midst of this," she went on bravely, "what *are* you going to do about your brother?"

"What am *I* going to do?"

"Right. He's family. You have to find a way to work

around this. Dean, do you really believe he's a bad person, that he does all this stuff out of some evil intent to spite you?"

He thought about it briefly, running his hand along her smooth thigh. The sight of her beside him, so close, made it difficult for him to concentrate on anything else. "No, I really don't. I guess the thing with Marilyn was a fluke—could have happened to anybody. I *think* that, Jennie, but I'm not sure I can feel it. And now, with you, I keep having this awful sense of déjà vu, seeing it about to happen again."

"Dean, it takes two. And if you truly believed what you say, you wouldn't be here with me now. You wouldn't be able to put your arms around me."

"I want to wrap you up and have you next to me, part of me," he whispered gently, drawing her even closer. The boat rocked them together for a sweet moment.

"But you can't keep me away from the world, or from other people. Think about it, Dean. Jim's not so bad. As a matter of fact, if you knew the way he looks up to you . . ." She smiled and touched his face, running her fingers along his cheekbone. "He said you had a deep soul, and that he was just a superficial cad."

Dean sighed, and then laughed a little. "Did he really say that?" He sounded genuinely amazed. "I don't want to distrust Jim. I wish I could get rid of the suspicion."

"But you can."

"For your sake, I'll try." He kissed her forehead softly, then worked his way down to her eyelids, which fluttered like young birds just hatched from the shell. "Just for you, Jennie," he whispered, almost too quietly for her to hear.

He was falling in love. He'd never been more certain of anything in his life. But how could he say it to her? The words simply wouldn't form in his mouth.

A rush of gladness swept over her, a tremendous feeling of tenderness toward this magnificent man. She kissed him again, brushing his full lips lightly with hers.

"Who wants a tuna sandwich?" The sound of Chris's voice came barreling down the passageway. Both Jennie and Dean burst out laughing, muffling the sounds in the pillow they shared.

"Yikes! They're back. Let's try to look normal," Jennie whispered, hopping out of bed.

"Do we have to?" Dean watched her for a minute, then realized they would have to put in an appearance sooner or later.

But neither of them felt at all normal as they casually strolled onto the main deck fifteen minutes later, hand in hand, suppressing giggles. The whole scene was too funny for anything resembling militarily correct behavior.

"Have a good talk?" Chris asked pointedly as the couple appeared at the top of the ladder.

"Excellent. Everything seems to be running smoothly now," Dean said with a perfectly serious expression on his face.

Jennie exploded with laughter.

"Aunt Jen, we're going to have lunch in the rowboat, and your friend can come, too. But you have to eat the sandwich I made for you, okay?" Timmy said excitedly.

"I wouldn't dream of eating another. Thanks, sweetie." She kissed the top of his head, then rumpled the wild hair that refused to stay in place.

"What can I do?" Dean asked. "How about making iced tea?" And with that, he nudged Molly out of the way and went to work, busily mixing up "his specialty"— a concoction of tea, mint, lemon, honey, and cinnamon—in the giant Thermos she gave him. To Jennie's amazement, the two started to compare chili recipes. She hadn't even suspected the guy could cook.

"Well, you look better, kid," Chris declared as he handed her a couple of oars and took two himself. Timmy went to loosen the winch that would let down the over-sized lifeboat from the side of the houseboat.

"I feel a lot better. Sorry we had to come down and unload the *sturm und drang* on you guys, though." She lent a hand, and together they worked the ropes to move the boat down to the waterline.

"I've been waiting to see you happy, Jen," her brother said solemnly. "I don't mean buried-in-work happy, either. I mean like other people do it, the folks like me with nice settled homes and families."

"Settled? You wouldn't want to see me settled, would you?" she scoffed. "Not wacky, high-flying Jennie?" But inside, something shifted as she repeated the word.

"We're ready if you are," Molly called down the passage. Dean was lugging a huge picnic basket that looked as though it contained provisions for a week.

"Then let's hoist anchor." Chris lifted his son into the boat, and Jennie jumped in to take the basket from Molly. When everyone was ensconced, Chris handed out the oars and pushed off against the side of the large boat.

It was a perfect day for a row. The sun made the water into a glasslike cover, and the screech of gulls around them was a suitable accompaniment to the trip. There was a smell of sand and surf in the air, the kind of scent that reminded all of them of childhood summers, of goofing-off days when there was nowhere special to go and nothing to do but have fun.

They passed a few more houseboats dotted along the shoreline, and then they were off, heading out to Timmy's favorite cove, about two miles distant. The blue of the sky wasn't as deep as that of Dean's eyes, but Jennie loved it anyway. Right now, she was in love with everything and everyone.

"Now, we have to have some teamwork here," Chris grumbled, acting the captain as usual. "I want crisp, even strokes and feathering only when everyone else is. We're bound over that way, which means some ducking and bobbing around those big rocks. All right, crew! Heave, one! Heave, two!"

"Why don't we take a starboard tack and go about?" Dean suggested. He was not used to being "crew" and apparently didn't have the knack of keeping his mouth diplomatically shut.

There was silence in the boat, and then Chris said, "Because we always go this way, that's why. You have any objections?"

"Oh, for heaven's sake, Chris!" Molly laughed, breaking the tension. "The man's perfectly right. We've been going the long way to that cove for years. And on a hot day, it's a real slog," she explained to Jennie over her shoulder.

Chris mumbled something into his beard and then shrugged. "Come about if you want. We'll try his way."

Jennie's heart sank as she imagined the confrontation about to take place between Dean and her brother. Two captains battling out the logistics of the navigation were not going to make for a delightful trip.

"Daddy, you're all wet. Dean knows better," Timmy chided his father.

"That's not true, Tim," Dean said at once. "I was just venturing an opinion, and since I've never been here before, I was out of line. Your dad probably has some very good reasons for going the other way. I have an idea: Let's go his way there and my way home. How about it?"

Jennie smiled at Dean's broad back and kept in rhythm with the pull of his powerful arms. She admired him all the more for making peace and keeping his ego out of the matter—especially because this was her family, the people who mattered most to her. If he could get along with Chris—another forceful personality—perhaps he could find a way to get along with his own brother. At least, she hoped he could.

The cove was covered with underbrush so thick that

it would have required a machete to get their little craft through it. So instead, the two men moored the boat to a fallen tree and they all crossed their fingers, hoping that a huge monsoon wouldn't swamp the boat while they were eating their lunch. They stowed the oars, and Molly grabbed the overstuffed basket. Then they began the arduous process of ducking through bushes and briers to get to the other side, the "paradise" side, as Timmy called it.

"You follow us, Aunt Jennie. We'll show you." Timmy darted ahead, his parents close on his heels, which left Jennie and Dean alone. He grasped her hand, then brought it to his cheek.

"Let's try to get marooned here after lunch," he suggested mischievously. "I've never made love on a desert island before." He grinned.

And it was a desert island movie location if ever Jennie had seen one. She wondered how similar their isolation in space would be to this. The two of them alone, floating around eating their prepackaged, dehydrated food, doing their work, strapping themselves in for the night, and bringing home with them an experience they could tell their grandchildren about—an experience people all over the world would discuss.

Their grandchildren? Watch it, girl, she cautioned herself, walking close to Dean, her hip bumping comfortably against his. You may be in love with the man, but he said he was a slow study. Nothing's guaranteed. And yet, she couldn't help seeing them as a couple, as two people who'd been searching long enough and now had found something very precious. In a way, this top-secret mission was even more frightening than it had been initially; so much was at stake, personally as well as scientifically and politically. She and Dean were two little cogs in the giant wheel of a great master plan, but they also had a relationship. What was it going to be like when they were the focus of public scrutiny?

"Here's the spot," Molly called back to them. They caught up hurriedly, but not before Dean had captured her behind a clump of bushes for a very long and very exciting kiss. When they arrived at the picnic area where Timmy and his father had already spread out the blanket and utensils, Jennie was still trying to regain her composure.

"Dig in," Molly insisted, handing sandwiches all around. She poured iced tea, and Jennie noticed that she avoided looking at the two lovers, who were exceptionally quiet and not particularly capable of unwrapping their own tin foil.

"I like that painting of the tug hanging in the guest room," Dean ventured when he realized that he and Jennie were being a bit unsociable, just mooning at each other.

Chris's eyes lit up. There was nothing he needed more than praise. "Working boats are my specialty. Historical scenes, naval battles, that kind of thing. No rag boats."

"That's sailboats to you," Molly explained with a laugh. "Chris hates nothing so much as a three-masted schooner in full sail setting off into the sunset."

"Barf!" Timmy added with a silly grin on his face.

"You've been taught well by your dad, I see," Dean observed, giving Timmy a playful poke.

"You're the flyer, right?" Chris asked Dean cautiously.

"You got it."

"And you're going up on this mission, too, huh? Whatever got you into the field?"

Jennie was pleased at what seemed to be Chris's genuine interest.

"I fell in love with jets at an early age. Can't seem to shake the feeling that I belong more in the sky than I do on earth. It's a kind of pull—the way you have to live on the water, I guess. But Jennie and I, we're somewhere off in the stratosphere."

And with that, he took the sandwich out of her hand

and pulled her to him, depositing a soft kiss on top of her head. She closed her eyes, wanting the perfection of this day and this grouping of wonderful people never to end.

"You two are real goners," Timmy said in a sorrowful tone. He clucked and shook his head, oblivious to the laughter all around him.

- *10* -

SOMEHOW THEY GOT through that last week. There were briefings, simulations, and debriefings; there was flight and landing; there was intensive study of the *Liberator*'s systems and instruments. Jennie came home every night dizzy, mouthing little reminders about where to put her feet during takeoff or how to eat properly aboard the shuttle.

"They won't give us anything gassy to eat," Dean said one night as they sat over a big pot of chili and some strong red wine at his house. "If you eat too fast and immediately start working at something strenuous, your meal can come back up on you. Peristalsis doesn't work so well without gravity." He winked, licking some of the chili off her fingers.

They'd been alternating nights at each other's house, and though they were sometimes too tired to make it through dinner, they were never too zonked to fall into each other's arms at every opportunity. Maybe it was the starkness of the kind of work they did, but lovemaking had become an oasis in their desert. They were no sooner in one house or another before Dean began backing her into corners or surprising her as she stood in the kitchen making a salad. She was the same with him, leaping on him as he lay dozing on the couch after a meal or tickling him awake in the early morning hours before they had to go to work.

Things were idyllic, she thought that week before the shoot. Were they too peaceful, too content with each other? There was no competition, no vying for first place, but instead, a quiet acceptance of each other and the work they would be doing together. Although none of the other astronauts on the shoot had yet been informed of the isolation program, Dean and Jennie had at least an hour a day alone together, working out specific details of the module deployment. As to what they'd be doing up there for three weeks, well, NASA seemed to be leaving a lot to them—and to chance.

Dean still had some flying time left to get in. That Thursday night before the shoot, he took off in heavy cloud cover, and Jennie watched him from the tower. He went through his paces for an hour, and finally, after one last somersault and triple spin, he brought the baby in for a perfect three-point landing. Exhausted as he was, he just didn't let go of his control. Not ever.

"Still trying to beat yourself at your own game, aren't you?" she teased.

"Stop griping. You're perfect all the time; I'm only perfect when you're watching," he said.

"Untrue!"

"Hey, Jennie, I want to hear you say you're good and you know it." Dean grabbed her around the waist and maneuvered her into a deserted corner of the hangar, where he proceeded to show her that daredevil flying only egged him on to a variety of other extraordinary physical feats.

"Dean, really! Someone's going to come over here and get the shock of his life," she whispered when they heard a group of returning pilots trooping through the vast space toward them.

"What if they do? C'mon, say it!"

"Oh, can it!"

"Repeat after me: I'm good!"

"Okay, for heaven's sake! I'm good. I'm great. As a matter of fact, I'm as good an astronaut as you are!" She yelled the last aloud.

He clapped a hand over her mouth as she struggled with him for footing. "Well, I didn't mean for you to go overboard on this."

"Why, you—!" She lunged at him and managed, after only a few minutes of wrestling, to pin him to the floor. "Give up?"

"Oh, all right. You cheated, but I concede. You're great, and you're also as strong as an ox, you little beast." He rose up on his elbows and studied her catlike face, the high cheekbones now glowing with an inner warmth. "I swear," he breathed, "if you didn't get more beautiful this week."

"Aw, shucks, mister," she said, getting up and giving him a hand. "T'ain't nothin'."

But she was more than pleased with the attention. It had been so long since anyone told her what she looked like that her self-image had dimmed like a fading light bulb. For all Dean's reticence, for all his inability to make his feelings known, he had a sixth sense about what she craved, what she needed. His hands on her were knowing, searching out the hidden places that made her tingle and shiver with delight. His mouth was sometimes tender with her, sometimes strong and demanding. It varied as rapidly as her moods.

"Jen, someone called in a message for you!" One of the guys in the office came rushing up just as she and Dean were about to walk into the parking lot.

"Oh, thanks, Tom."

Dean waited patiently while she scanned the note.

When he saw her face fall, he put an arm around her, drawing her close. "No bad news, I hope."

"No, uh ... Dean, it's Jim." She said it quietly, expecting the worst. Which was exactly what she got.

"Why, that ... I'm going to give that guy a piece of my—" He was off and running for his car.

She was hot on his heels. "Stop it! Will you just wait a second! You promised you were going to get rid of that jealous attitude. Can't you see how unreasonable you're being? Give the guy a break! Dean, you don't even know where he is. Don't be an idiot!"

She could see the fury mounting in him, leaving no room for thought or patience. He revved the engine, not even looking at her. "You have to deal with this without flying off the handle every time it happens. For godsake, can't you see what you're doing?" she blurted out.

He looked at her, another man now, not the one who had spent the weekend getting to know her family and the rest of the week getting to know her.

"Why should I give him the benefit of the doubt? Jennie, isn't it obvious to you by now? Whether you know it or not, he's interested in you. Once again he decides to romance my woman with complete impunity. I should have told him off years ago, but I'm going to take care of it now. And don't you tell me how to—"

"My God, I've never met such a pigheaded man! All right, let's go see him. If you're right, we can both tell him off. And if you're wrong, you'd better have a damned good apology ready. Well, what are you waiting for? The message said he'd meet me at my house," she said, getting into the car with him. "Go on," she urged when he sat grimly, staring at the steering wheel.

"I don't want you involved."

"Oh, you don't! I think you still have a lot to learn about me—you know that? I *am* involved. Don't you dare shut me out or try to protect me from something you think I can't handle."

He listened to her intensity and finally nodded, revving the engine and racing toward their destination. Neither of them spoke. Finally they saw the car parked by the side of Jennie's house, and the figure seated behind the wheel was waiting.

"What damned gall!" Dean muttered. His rugged face was crease with anger and bitterness. Jennie hated to see the spark in his deep blue eyes turn to dull, fixed anguish.

"Look, don't go off half cocked and take a swing at him. If you do, and you're wrong, you'll never forgive yourself. How about trying it my way?"

His answer was a shrug. Evidently the competitiveness in him was too fierce for anything else. When it came to matters he considered vital, he wouldn't let her in, and that angered her. Furiously tearing out of the car, he began stalking toward Jim. Jennie walked calmly behind him, disappointed that he simply wouldn't—or couldn't—acknowledge anyone else's competence. She had no idea what she wanted to say or do, but then, this wasn't exactly a controlled scientific experiment where she could gauge every move.

"Well, at last I get to see the two of you together!" Jim had gotten out of his car to approach them and put his arm around his brother's shoulder. He looked surprised and hurt when Dean brushed it off, glowering at him.

"What's gotten into you, pal?" Jim asked, looking concerned.

"Your brother has a crazy idea that you're pursuing me. Would you like to set the record straight?" Jennie stood beside Dean, feeling the anger emanating from him.

Jim looked puzzled at first, then somewhat saddened. "Is *that* it? I couldn't understand why you didn't return a single one of my phone calls this week, Dean. Look, this is a great woman you've got here, and I'd be out of my mind if I didn't think she was pretty terrific . . . but what's yours is yours."

Dean's face didn't soften. He simply said, "I've kept

silent about something for a lot of years, Jim. Was I right to do that?"

"About Marilyn?" He looked sheepish.

"That's right," Dean said tersely.

"Well," Jim said, "I guess I was just so flattered that she'd even consider me after being engaged to you, I couldn't bring myself to discourage her."

Dean looked amazed but didn't comment.

"That was a mistake. A big one. But I was young and I was selfish and I didn't know the meaning of important relationships. I'm sorry, Dean. Genuinely. I have been for a long time." Then he chuckled uneasily. "But look at it this way, pal. If you'd actually gone ahead and married Marilyn, you might never have met this gem here." He looked fondly at Jennie.

Jennie was somewhat chagrined to realize that she'd underestimated the long-standing rift between the two brothers. She reflected that Dean wasn't the only competitive one in his family—nor the only one who kept his mouth shut at the wrong times!

In the face of Dean's silence, Jim continued, "I guess I've been flirting around for so long, it didn't occur to me to shut it off with Jennie. But I didn't really mean anything by it. Especially since, well . . . the real reason I came by is that I wanted to tell you my terrific news." He grinned at them. "Believe it or not, I'm engaged."

Jennie thought she hadn't heard right. "Engaged to be married?"

"You remember Carole Jasper, don't you, Dean? I must admit I've been after her for a while, calling her in New York all the time, sending her flowers, pestering the hell out of her. She kept putting me off, so I never said anything—I didn't want to brag till I was sure. Well, last night she finally said the magic word. I hope the two of you will be dancing at my wedding next March."

Jennie rubbed the back of her neck, easing out the knot. So that was the reason for those phone calls every time she saw him! The poor guy, so desperate for someone to love him.

Dean shook his head, then gave a slight, self-deprecating laugh. "You're incredible," he told his brother.

"I know I am. But what can I do? That's me. So, anyway, you can rest easy from here on." Jim paused, then said hopefully, "Truce?"

Jennie looked from one man to the other, seeing a new understanding grow between them. Dean said nothing for a moment more; then he thrust out his hand, and Jim took it. "Truce," Dean agreed. "Listen," he added grudgingly, "I hope this one works out. Don't scrap anything that's potentially important to you, Jim." He looked hard at Jennie and took her by both hands. "I know what I'm talking about."

"My kid brother giving me advice!" Jim grinned. "Yeah, well, he's always known better. Hey, I'm sorry we all couldn't have gotten together last week. Next time you're in the city, you be sure to give me a call, though, okay? We'll make it a foursome. Jennie, best of luck in your work. Both of you. Hope the shoot's perfect."

The three of them stood there outside her house as a light rain began to fall. Jennie was so aware of the fragile bond between people, sometimes stretched to an unbearable breaking point.

She extended her hand to Jim, and he shook it. Then Dean came to his brother, as absorbed as she'd ever seen him. He put his arms around Jim and embraced him fiercely. They stood there locked together for a moment. Then Jim finally turned to leave.

"I'll be watching you on TV," was his parting shot. He got back into his car, started up the engine, and drove off cavalierly, a jaunty wave signifying that things were pretty much okay in his world.

"If that guy ever gets married, I'll eat a satellite," Dean muttered as they watched the car disappear down the road.

"It'd leave an awful lump in your stomach," she teased gently.

"You're right. And, come to think of it, he probably will marry her." He chuckled and put his arms around her tightly. "If I ever met a bigger flirt than my brother, it's Carole Jasper." He paused. "Can I have a kiss?" he asked softly. "I need one."

"It's yours," she told him gently, enfolding his large body in her slim arms and tilting her head back. If there was ever a time when she wanted to tell him she loved him . . . Soon, she thought.

"And for all you middle-of-the-night owls, this is Jerry the Jockey, bringing you all the hits, all the time. It's four A.M., folks, and if anyone out there is listening, it's supposed to be a foggy day in Houston town."

Jennie reached out a hand blindly and slapped the alarm button on her clock-radio so that Jerry the Jockey wouldn't be able to blast her and Dean out of bed with some godawful rock 'n' roll. They had to be at work in half an hour; the shoot was set for nine-fifteen, Florida time.

"Galvanize yourself, mister," she whispered, kissing him lightly. "There's a job to be done up there. Our country is counting on us."

"Ugh," he muttered, ungluing first one eye and then the other.

She showered quickly and left some food for Wings, who was too sleepy to raise her head from the bottom of the bed, where she always slept.

"Susan has the keys, and she'll be in every night to take care of you, sweetheart," Jennie told the cat, dropping a quick pat on her old, grizzled head. "Be good, and don't smell up the litter box too much. See you in three weeks."

She went outside to warm up the truck and wait for Dean. It was so still! She stopped a moment to listen to the morning. A few birds were up and singing, but it was still pitch black, so she couldn't see where they were. She heard the scurry of a squirrel darting through a hedge, then silence. No one around. She climbed into her truck, yawning, and turned on the headlights. A thick film of fog covered everything.

"This better burn off," she muttered to herself. "Otherwise, it's no go."

"Okay, Jennie, full speed ahead. But without the speed." Dean's hair was still wet from his shower, but he seemed very much awake now, more so than she. "Keep your wits about you," he told her as she switched on her fog lights and started off at a crawl.

The sky grew lighter as she approached Clear Lake City, but the sparse traffic along the turnpike was slowed almost to a halt. Jennie turned on the radio to Jerry the Jockey.

"I'm telling you," the man said, "it's pea soup out there, folks. Never seen anything like it. Not that I can see anything."

"Will you look at that!" Dean exclaimed. "That sun looks like the moon. Pretty strange." It did, too—a pale circle of silver peering blindly through the fog.

And then, everything disappeared. Jennie couldn't see her own lights ahead of her, let alone the road. Driving at five miles an hour, she squinted into the thick miasma. It could have been a Scottish moor out there, or the surface of the moon, for all she knew. The sun was trying to burn through, and here and there she could make out treetops, but otherwise the fog was impermeable. Not a road sign or a car visible, although she could hear from the honking around her that they weren't alone. It was an eerie feeling, steering through one fog bank only to be hit by another, thicker one. The road had vanished, and so had the traditional markers she always passed on the way to work. Luckily, several cars were turning onto Nasa Road 1, so she didn't miss it. The light at the end of the drive winked at her provocatively.

"Is that you, Dr. Jacobs? And Lieutenant Bradshaw?" asked the guard at the gate.

"None other," she confirmed. She could make out his peaked cap and the very top of the Mercury Redstone that sat at the entrance to the space center. Shepherd and Grissom had flown that baby in 1961. The very thought of the history they had made—and she would make in time—gave her goosebumps.

"Don't see how they can send you up in this," the guard clucked. "How can they even get you to Cape Kennedy?"

"Ah, that's for them to know and us to find out," Dean joked. "You ought to know by now, Smitty. It's all done with mirrors. Nobody's ever really been up there." He pointed heavenward, and the guard laughed.

"Well, kids, good luck. Bon voyage and all that."

Jennie nodded and drove on. But she had her doubts. Flying to Florida seemed out of the question right now.

They checked in at Building 2 and went to their separate dressing rooms to don the fire-retardant jumpsuits they'd be wearing on the flight. Jennie and Darlene had been fitted with silver-white ones; the guys had olive-drab green. The big space suits she and Dean would wear for the module deployment were already on board the *Liberator*, which had been shipped down to Florida the previous week.

The press room was a total zoo, as it usually was before a shoot. No one walking into the room cold would ever have assumed it was five o'clock on a morning so thick with fog you could spread it on bread and cut it.

Dan Abrams, the PR director, was rushing around, trying to carry on three conversations at once. All the lights of his telephone were blinking.

"Are we going? We're not really going, are we?" Rob Callahan led the procession into the office. He looked frazzled, but not as much as James Donadio, the payload specialist from Monmouth Mechanicals. Although these specialists had as much or more training as any of the astronauts, they were still civilians, and very wet behind the ears.

"You really think Dean and I can get that dinosaur up in this weather?" asked flight commander Jeff Davis.

"Hey, forget the shuttle! What I want to know is, who's going to risk his neck to fly us tc Florida?" asked Darlene. She was standing by the doorway with Jennie, who was all set to be sent back to change and go to work in the simulator.

"I am," came a voice from the back of the room. A few flashbulbs went off as the newspaper and magazine people recorded their stories. The TV cameras rolled, and a reporter rushed up to the man who had spoken— a NASA flight specialist, a Navy jet pilot who was called in only for the toughest assignments.

"They're going to regret this," Dean murmured to Jennie. The six of them were led out of the room, handed some last-minute briefings, and bussed out to the airfield, followed by at least four camera crews. The fog was lifting a little, but no one in his right mind would have called these clear flying conditions. They were about to enter the tiny plane when Peter Reinhardt came rushing up, Steve Akins and Ann Lorge right behind him.

"Good luck, you guys—and women," Peter told them heartily. "I know we're going to have a great one." He winked at Jennie. "You bring back some good results, okay?" he told her.

"I'll try, sir," she said, her voice steady and calm. She didn't want any camera to register the bubbling turmoil and frenzy inside her, because the world expected to see the cookie-cutter astronaut, the icy-calm personality with all the right stuff. She wanted to appear just the way Dean always did: completely in control. But inside, she was roiling. Part of it was disbelief and part was complete and utter hysteria. She was going up! "I'm sure we all will."

At five-thirty on the nose they took off, the pilot

steering them high above the dense cloud banks. Jennie and Dean, sitting close together near the plane's tail, held hands and didn't speak. Jeff was giving them the eleventh-hour plans, and it was their job to concentrate. Jennie's mind felt too full to contain anything other than her own amazement. Who would have ever thought that a small-town Wisconsin girl, a doctor of sports physiology, would be winging her way toward one of the most unusual missions ever flown?

They were deposited at the foot of the *Liberator,* a huge aircraft consisting of two solid-fuel rocket boosters, an external tank, and the orbiter—a unit comparable in size to a standard DC-9—where the crew would work and live. About thirty men and women wearing white coats or blue NASA work suits were milling around, checking out the craft for any kinks or evident problems. When at last the three computer experts emerged from the orbiter with thumbs up, the word was go. They were ready.

"Seven-thirty, and I feel I've been up for hours." Jennie grimaced, suppressing a yawn.

"In a minute, you're going to be the most *un*-tired you've ever been," Rob told her.

"Just a sec!" Darlene looked frantic as she started for one of the ground trucks. "Don't leave without me!"

"What's with her?" Jeff asked in annoyance.

"I . . . uh . . . think it's a call of nature," James Donadio told him in a hushed tone. "Nerves, you know."

Dean grinned and took the opportunity to steer Jennie away from the rest of the group. "How're you doing?" he asked solicitously.

"Oh, about to jump out of my skin, I guess. I brought this, for luck," she said, retrieving his Yankees baseball cap from her back pocket.

He clucked at her in mock annoyance. "Not standard NASA issue. Don't let anyone see it." Stealthily, under cover of fog, he took the cap and unzipped her jumpsuit down the front, down to the cleavage that rose up out of her black lace bra. "Store that, would you, Jen?" He tucked the cap under her arm. His warm hand was on her skin only briefly, and then he'd zipped her up again.

"Let's get this show on the road! You two stragglers, come on!"

They heard, rather than saw, Jeff Davis stomping up the steps toward the orbiter in his heavy work boots. As they approached, they saw Rob and Darlene start up, and then Donadio. They were at the steps in an instant, ready to receive the handshakes and good wishes of the ground personnel.

"Well, look at this!" one of the mechanics shouted. "It's clearing! Look at that pretty sight."

The fog was rolling off as if it had been pushed by a giant hand. Underneath, a sky as bright and beautiful as Jennie had ever seen smiled at them and at the work they would do that day.

"A good omen," Dean pronounced, ushering her up the steps.

And then she was inside, taking her place and strapping in on the flight deck behind Jeff and Dean. The other three were already down below them on middeck, getting ready. Jeff's communicators were on now, and the closed-circuit TV screens above them showed the frantic pace of work in the mission control center. They could all sense the electricity in the air, the palpable feeling that something out of the ordinary was about to take place.

"*Liberator,* this is Kennedy." Abigail Sarasin, Capcom once again, sounded pretty excited for someone who still wasn't flying. "Hear you've solved the weather problem."

"Affirmative. That's go-ahead, I take it," Dean responded.

"We have liftoff in minus thirty-nine and counting. Set your watches, boys and girls."

Jennie smiled to herself, securing her straps a little more tightly. Was this really happening? She prepared the computer information for takeoff as Jeff and Dean arranged their flight plans and instructions on the counter beneath the six forward windows of the cabin. The clock on the wall above them showed the countdown, which was imminent.

"I don't believe this," she muttered as the minutes ticked off.

"You'd better, kid," Jeff said with a smile. "Look at me—calm, cool, collected."

"With his nails bitten to the quick and dying for a cigarette," Dean chided him. "The man's teeth are even chattering, Jennie. I can hear them over here."

The easy camaraderie helped them all. As prepared as they were, as competent as they felt, they were all experiencing a certain terror of the unknown. But when Abby began the countdown, the computers started clicking the time off, and the boosters were actually fired, there was no time for anything but total attention to detail. Everyone had a job to do.

"Roll systems, go!" Abby's voice came through clearly as the computers showed the *Liberator* in position, about to lift off. "Nine—eight—seven—six—five... engine arm ascent. Beautiful, team! Four—three—two—one—zero."

They were sucked back in their chairs by the mighty power of the craft's upward surge. The intensity of gravity's pull caused Jennie to close her eyes and involuntarily curl into herself. She felt small and weak in the face of the incredible force working on her.

"And we have liftoff," Jeff said when he got his breath.

"Liftoff is affirmative. Thirty-six feet per second up."

"Pitch over," Dean said. They stopped buffeting and felt the pull of gravity lessen slightly.

"Ten seconds," Abby stated.

"Pitch over is good. That's affirmative. Auto-ignition," Jeff said.

What happened next occurred so quickly that Jennie didn't even have time to think. A rancid smell, like that of rubber burning, permeated the cabin.

"Smoke! What is this?" she heard Dean shout before the whole place was inundated with fumes. Jeff was coughing too hard to catch his breath and tell mission control.

"Abort!" Jennie said in a loud, clear voice. "Dean, tell her we need an emergency landing!"

"What the hell? It's the heat-shield tiles, dammit! One of them's on fire!" She heard him cough, and then there was silence. She had only one thought, and that was getting to him, saving him. She knew the others were in trouble, but to her, Dean was the most precious cargo they were carrying.

Daring the impossible, she unstrapped herself and crawled on her hands and knees to the flight deck. It was only a few short steps, but it seemed like miles to Jennie. Jeff had passed out and was sprawled in his seat. She couldn't see Dean through the smoke, but she could hear him moan.

"Oh, God, Abby!" she screamed into the communicator. "Get us down! I can't see the clock, but I calculate that we've got only two and a half minutes." During the first four minutes of flight, the orbiter could be safely returned to the runway. If they waited any longer, the maneuver would be more complex and would take forever. And one thing they couldn't afford right now was time.

"I've got you in range," Abby assured her. "Keep to your stations."

But there was no way she could get back to her seat. "Dean! Dean! Are you all right?" Jennie cried, struggling toward him. And then the force of the backward pull of the craft threw her to the floor. Her head hit metal, and she was out cold.

- 11 -

MISSION CONTROL HAD them down in less than the two and a half minutes Jennie had specified, and even before they landed, ground crews had mammoth hoses trained on the fiery craft.

"One damned heat shield," a technician sighed as the last puff of smoke died. "What happened to the sprinkler system, for heaven's sake?"

Dean regained consciousness just as the hatch was being pried open. He opened his eyes, coughing, and was immediately aware of the woman he loved lying half on top of him, a thin trickle of blood showing through the tousled auburn curls on the right side of her head. A nasty bump had already sprouted.

"Oh, sweetheart, wake up, will you?" He kissed her, hoping for the Prince Charming effect on Snow White, but got no result. When the medics rushed in with oxygen masks, he waved them away. "Treat Dr. Jacobs first," he insisted, allowing the men to lift her slight body and put it on a stretcher. "I suspect a concussion. And then get Commander Davis out. I'll check on the others on middeck."

"Sorry, Bradshaw. You get on a stretcher, too," said a laconic black medic in his early thirties. "We know you guys eat nails for breakfast, but orders are orders. No heroics."

Dean, much to his chagrin, let them carry him off the aircraft. The three on middeck were woozy, but they hadn't been overcome by the smoke, so that left only Jennie and Jeff in need of immediate treatment.

They came out to a hail of flashbulbs. The medics had to fight off the reporters, and the one PR man at the scene was going out of his mind trying to keep order. The crew was taken immediately to the infirmary to be treated for smoke inhalation.

"Put us in the same room," Dean demanded as soon as they were inside the hospital. He took Jennie's hand and wouldn't let go.

"Lieutenant, we have certain rules and regulations here, and—" the officious nurse began, waving her clipboard at him.

"Scrap 'em. I say we get the same room." And with that, he swung his legs off the stretcher and got up, ignoring the feelings of nausea and dizziness that threatened to overcome him.

"Hey, what's going on?" Jennie's voice was faint and weak, but the feisty tone was unmistakable. She tried to raise her head, but Dean settled her back on the stretcher.

"You, young lady, have a big bump on your head. Stay still."

"Oh, no!" she wailed, suddenly much stronger. "If it's a concussion, they'll ground me. I won't be able to fly!"

"Will you shut up?" was Dean's loving response.

They kept Jennie overnight for observation, despite her protests. Everyone else was given a little oxygen before being discharged and told to lay low for a day or so. Dean stayed with her until midnight, in blatant disregard of the infirmary policy, and was back at eight the next morning to pick her up.

"Are we going home?" she asked as they strolled out the front door into the Florida sunshine. She'd been given a clean bill of health and told to apply ice packs to the bump on her head. But at least it wasn't a concussion.

"No, apparently they want us to stick around here, get in a little more training, and try for another shoot next Thursday. Can you believe it? The sprinkler system's on the fritz, and all of us nearly buy it. What idiots!"

She shivered a little in the heat, realizing how close they all had come. And then she stopped where she was and took his face in her hands, a look of love so intense on her face that he couldn't turn away. Her hazel eyes spoke before she did.

"I want you so much," she said quietly.

"Honey, you're supposed to go to bed, but the way *we* go to bed may be a little too much for you," he teased.

"It's the best medicine," she replied, grinning.

They took one of the NASA cars and drove to the motel on the outskirts of the center where the crew had been ensconced. Dean got his key from reception while she waited, and then they zoomed to his assigned room, both of them giggling like kids.

"This is wicked. Making love in the middle of the day."

"What do you mean, middle? It's only zero-nine-hundred hours, Houston time, darling." He grinned, closing the door behind them. But the smile became a tender glance as he took her in his arms and pulled her close. "If anything had happened to you . . ." he murmured into her hair.

"You were the one in danger," she insisted, kissing his cheek, his nose, his eyelids. "I was petrified when I saw you conked out. Just a few more of those noxious fumes and—"

"You should never have unstrapped—you know that,"

he scolded her lightly. He lifted her gently and carried her to the bed.

She reached up for the zipper on his jumpsuit and playfully eased it down, releasing the soft golden chest hairs that shone like polished brass in the bright morning sunlight. "Well, cowboy, so much for space flight."

"Wait a sec. The journey is yet to come," he whispered. He tugged at her zipper and began peeling the suit off her carefully, stopping as he went to kiss and caress each exposed inch. Starting with her gleaming white shoulder, he progressed downward, nuzzling her perfect breasts, taking each one out of its black lace nest and then, when she could hardly bear the wonderful promise of his hands on her, unhooking the bra and thrusting it aside. He proceeded to take each arm out of the jumpsuit and to nibble the alabaster flesh beneath gently and meticulously.

"I have to memorize all of you," he breathed huskily into her ear. "I need to know the location of every beauty mark, every vein, every curve."

"It's all right," she assured him, her fingers tracing circles around the nipples of his muscular chest, "we have all the time in the world."

But as he eased her suit all the way off her, it suddenly occurred to him that she was wrong, that regardless of how long they lived, they couldn't afford to waste a precious minute of their time together. He wanted her now, completely and forever. "God, Jennie, how I love you!"

She closed her eyes to the warmth of his breath, the meaning of his words. Never in her life had she been happier, had she ever felt that paradise was as near as a simple touch, a bold statement of commitment. This man, this exceptional person who had given her so much in such a short time, was in fact the beginning and end of everything for Jennie. And as long as they were together, nothing could be wrong.

"Hold me," she begged him, pulling at his clothing, insisting that he be as naked and vulnerable as she. When finally they lay together, flank against flank, they marveled in the excitement of being so close and of having the time to relish it. They didn't move at first, just let their fingers interlace and grip as their mouths joined in wonderful harmony, creating the purest song either of them had ever sung.

Then he drew back, awestruck at his luck and happiness, and began to work his way down her smooth form. His hands and mouth forged a searing path of hot kisses, which grew deeper and more intense as he progressed lower and lower. She moaned, growing frenzied under his slow, thorough devotion to her body. She cried out for him, urging him on.

He did everything she wanted—he would do anything she asked—and she arched under him, raising her hips and holding tight to him, trying to get closer, even closer.

He would have played like this for hours, prolonging their pleasure, but she couldn't wait. She edged herself around on the bed and reached for him. He let her take the lead and offered himself to her attentions. She stroked and lapped at him eagerly, honing his energies to a peak, then raising them even higher.

"Please, Dean, I need you inside me," she crooned, drawing him into her. His body was a tight rock shield that protected her from all evil. As long as he covered her, she was safe and secure.

But the delight of that safety soon changed as he moved within her, becoming a white-hot force that unraveled the edges of her mind and soul and left them in tatters. She was his, completely and irrevocably, and that would never change.

"I love you!" she cried out as they raced blindly toward the summit of their passion. "Oh, Dean, I love you!" she moaned into his chest, holding him to her with a strength he never realized she possessed. His love for her spilled over, and he groaned as he met her intensity and they climbed further upward together. They both clung to one rising star, which was the feeling that had blossomed and bloomed between them. They were weightless, floating, landmarks of love high above the barren earth.

Slowly they returned, easing back onto the pillows, their hot bodies spent and tired on the beige coverlet. Their hearts beat a wild rhythm that gradually quieted to a patent throbbing, and their breathing was softer, completely contented now. Jennie's arms were around his neck when she sighed with pleasure and snuggled into the nooks and crannies of his incredible, muscular body. They slept then, and slept soundly.

It was late afternoon when Dean opened his eyes and realized where he was. He hugged her to him, and she smiled in her sleep, saying something that sounded like "applesauce." He laughed gently, then extricated his arms from her so that he could get up and go to the bathroom. When he came back, she was sitting up in bed, waiting for him.

"We must have crash-landed," she said, not at all self-conscious about the way he was looking at her, with such love, such fervor.

"Nope. I'd call it a three-point landing," he corrected her, coming to sit by her side. She tried to get out of bed, but he held her back, pinning her against the pillows.

"Now I know you don't feel incapacitated, but I promised those meatheads I'd make you rest for a few days. You have to be in shape for Thursday, you know. So I think I'll pamper you a bit."

"What? No debriefings? No more tests?"

"Not for you. But I'm expected over there sometime tomorrow."

"Tell me something." She laced her fingers around his neck.

"Name it."

"Is this going to work out? Two crazy, driven astronauts like us? Two people who constantly feel they have to make the grade?" She knew the answer, but she needed to hear it from him.

"Baby, we'll make it work. I've never wanted anything so much in my life," he said intensely. And when he kissed her this time, there was not a doubt in her mind that he meant what he said.

They went up on Thursday. The countdown was smooth, with no interruptions and no malfunctions. Peter Reinhardt, who'd flown in from Houston for the shoot, decided that Jennie was to be relieved of all duties until liftoff, so she was forced to just wait, idly, restlessly.

There was hardly any less excitement on the day of the shoot, because each time up was a new experience for everyone. And, having come so close the last time, everyone was on his or her toes.

The solid-fuel rocket boosters fired, and the winged craft lifted gracefully off the launching pad, starting for the heavens. Jennie could picture mission control holding their collective breath, watching the event on television as well as on the plotting and tracking chart that took up one entire wall of the room.

"They're up!" they heard Peter declare as the *Liberator* crossed a glorious rainbow in the sky and rose over the Atlantic Ocean. Abigail, the Capcom, sounded happier than she'd been in quite a while. "You look good from here, guys," she said through her microphone. "How does it feel?"

Jeff Davis, completely recovered from the other day, grinned into the closed-circuit TV screen. "Sure is pretty up here."

Jennie couldn't take her eyes off the scene out the nearest window. The earth seemed to fall away from her as the G-forces accelerated and pushed her back in her chair. She had never seen such blue, nor had she ever imagined the speed with which everything familiar to her would vanish. The odd thing was, they hardly seemed to be moving. Suspended in the void, the world receded from them; the crew was alone above the atmosphere. She glanced over at Dean and found him staring at her. Their eyes locked and danced a moment; then they returned soberly to the matter at hand.

"Houston, they've passed the tower. Switching over," Abigail told her counterpart back in Texas, who was waiting for his cue. Mission control at the Kennedy Center monitored the shuttle only through liftoff. After that, all systems were controlled by Houston, where Abby would be flown later that morning so she could take over as Capcom.

"Solid-fuel boosters cease firing," Jeff reported as the gigantic tanks dropped away and fell into the sea.

"I read you," said Houston.

"We are up sixty nautical miles and climbing."

"Give me your status on programs, Jennie."

"We're on target, sir. No indication of any trouble," she told the ground personnel, tearing herself away from the view. "Lord, is this gorgeous!"

"Aw, they all say that," came the response.

Dean looked at the TV screen over his right shoulder. "You scoff, mister, but you've never had the privilege. Believe us, it's out of this world."

"I should hope so!" the guy joked.

"External tank separation," Jeff stated. "Ready for orbit insertion."

They were traveling faster now, just a lightweight piece of metal in the vast blue depths. Unencumbered by the assist rockets and tanks, they were now free to start into their orbit around the earth, one hundred fifty nautical miles up. It was almost too amazing to contemplate.

Jeff turned away from his panel and grinned at Dean and Jennie. "I guess we're airborne. Signing off, Houston." He flipped the toggles, severing television contact with the ground. The radio communicator was still configured for transmission, but they wouldn't be picked up until they passed over the next tracking station, which was Madrid. Jeff turned away from his panel and nodded to the other two. "Want to start on the activity plan for the day?"

And then Jennie felt something very peculiar. Her arms started floating up of their own accord. Even a minor readjustment in her chair made her aware of the lack of gravity.

"Who's first to float?" They heard Rob's voice from down on middeck. "Hey, I like this."

This was it, then. After years of research on weightlessness, Jennie was finally able to see what it actually felt like. In fact, as she undid her harness and stayed very still, she was surprised to find that nothing happened. Only when she leaned forward slightly was she carried away, her arms and legs curling inward slightly like the limbs of a praying mantis. Suddenly, she was moving slowly around in a circle, and she didn't stop until she collided with Dean.

"Get me a screwdriver, would you, Jennie?" he asked, holding her briefly around the waist. "Wouldn't you know there'd be a panel loose? Tools are in that drawer over there."

The drawers along the length of the craft were set in upside down, so that things wouldn't fly up as soon as they were released from their Velcro closures. It was really quite ingenious.

"If you have everything you need," she said, floating it over to him, "I think I'd better get to work."

"I can spare you. Briefly," he added solemnly. Then, in a whisper, he added, "Can't wait till tomorrow so we can get out of this crowd."

She grinned and started down to middeck, where she was scheduled to assist Darlene and Rob in preparing the module for the following day's deployment. The rest of the crew had been informed at the last minute that both Dean and Jennie would be launched away from the shuttle, and the official word was that they were to perform weightlessness experiments alone for the next three weeks. The couple had received several meaningful looks from Rob, but the other members of the crew had taken the news in stride.

So now they went to work, Jennie on the computer and the other two on last-minute physical adjustments. As they tumbled lightly and carefully around the cabin, holding on to the various straps and footrests that were part of every shuttle's equipment, Jennie began to feel the strain of working without gravity. You had to be twice as meticulous about putting things in place, and even the effort of typing data into the computer seemed enormous.

"When do we eat?" Rob complained after two hours of their tedious chores.

Jennie checked her wristwatch, then plugged in the time and coordinates to her computer. "Old metal-brains here says we're allowed a snack now, but we've made only six orbits, Rob. You have to wait till we've gone around the world another twenty times for a whole gourmet meal."

"Hey, I'm so hungry I could eat a plastic bag," Darlene declared, winging her way over to the "kitchen" for their mid-morning treat.

"And you will, too," Rob replied.

They gathered up a few self-contained baggies of dehydrated items labeled "Peach Ambrosia" and "Prune Surprise" and carried them upstairs to the main deck.

"This one says to add two ounces of cold water," Jennie told the others, looking skeptically at the so-called food. "I have a feeling it should be eaten as is, though. A little water might just drown the exquisite flavor." She sniffed the plastic as though it contained a fine vintage wine and laughingly handed it to Jeff, who refused it.

"Not feeling so great. Dean, relieve me, would you?" the commander asked. "How's the head working, Jennie?"

"It's supposed to be all right," she told him, concerned. "Are you having motion sickness? Disorientation?"

"You got it." He floated past her and made his way down the staircase. The others looked after him pityingly.

"Donadio's been in and out of a fog since we took off. I strapped him into his bunk a while ago," Rob said. "That's two of us affected. How are you two doing?" he asked Dean and Jennie.

They both said they were feeling fine.

"Well, that's nice, because we wouldn't want your little experiment to be botched up by upset tummies, would we?" He gave them each a suggestive grin.

"What in the world are you talking about, Rob?" Darlene asked in annoyance.

"You do know what these two are going to be doing alone in that module, don't you?" Rob prodded Darlene. "I mean, I know what I'd do if I had the chance."

"You, my good man, have a filthy mind," Darlene told him, shoving him halfway across the cabin with a good-natured brush of her hand.

There was a rapid beeping on one of their consoles, letting them know that mission control wanted to talk with them. Dean answered immediately, switching the TV back on again.

"Roger, Houston. We read you. Can I do something for you?"

"You guys ready for a little fireside chat?" Abby asked.

"Well," Dean said, grinning into the camera, "you didn't waste any time. Didn't expect to see you till lunch."

"It's past lunch, Bradshaw. Look outside."

"It's pitch black out there—what do I know?"

She sighed in exasperation. "Hey, the President's on the phone. Want to say hi?"

Dean glanced at the others. "I think we're about to

perform, folks. Get those two malingerers on their feet."
He turned back to his communicator as Rob floated
downstairs to rescue the two sick men.

"Remember, the media's in on this, too. Put some
powder on your nose, will you, Bradshaw? We need these
shots."

Jennie's heart began pounding. It was difficult trying
to reconcile the job they were doing with the incredible
views out the window and with her giddy, excited feelings
about the experience she and Dean were going to share.

"We're ready, I guess," Dean said, looking back to
see Rob nearly hauling Jeff and Donadio up the steps.
They both appeared to be a bit green around the gills.

"I'm switching over to the White House," Abby told
him. And then, after a little crackling and buzzing, the
familiar voice of the President of the United States came
humming through the craft.

"Hello, all of you!" he said in a jovial tone.

"Hello, Mr. President." Jeff, as commander of the
flight, spoke first.

"Just wanted to wish you well and tell you how much
I appreciate what you're doing up there."

"We're thrilled to be here, Mr. President," Dean told
him.

"I'm sure *you're* thrilled, Lieutenant Bradshaw," the
President chuckled. "Who wouldn't be, in your shoes?"

Jennie turned red, even though she realized that no
one in the nation would get this private joke.

"And to the rest of you—Dr. Jacobs, Dr. Callahan,
Dr. McFadden, Mr. Donadio—all the best."

"Thank you, Mr. President," they murmured nearly
in chorus.

"See you in a few weeks; I'm inviting you all to lunch
at the White House. Signing off now."

They were quickly switched back to mission control,
and, after a quick talk with them, they once again severed
their contact with the ground.

"That was it? No drum rolls and trumpets? No startling

words of wisdom?" Darlene looked rather put out.

"Well, what do you want from the man? Einstein's theory of relativity? It's all show biz, sweetheart," Rob told her, sneaking an arm around her shoulder. She brusquely swung it off, causing him to spin wildly in space.

"Say, lunch at the White House! Not really something we've been trained for," Jennie remarked. "After three weeks of sucking food out of a plastic bag, I may be unfit for human company."

"Well, we'll just have to see about that, won't we?" Dean answered. "I'll let you know when you're out of line."

"Hey, in this environment, who can stay in line?" she joked, bobbing from one side of the cabin to the other.

"We'd better try," Jeff cut in. "Hey, folks, I hate to be a spoilsport, but we have a busy day tomorrow. How about a little work?"

They buckled down then and returned to their routine chores, all of which had been laid out for them weeks in advance. Jennie did everything efficiently and well, but she was still pretty starry-eyed. Anyone who looked at her would know that the cosmos had nothing on her.

- *12* -

Personal Flight Log, 034.25 hours. Liberator *module:*

Didn't get much sleep last night. Who could, zipped up in those mesh hammocks, slung under a crawlspace so we won't float free? It's impossible to tell whether you're lying down or standing up. And it drives me wild to be so close to him and have no contact at all, to behave as if he's just a colleague, when here we are at work together, and work just happens to be hundreds of miles above the earth.

Dean and I suited up first thing, as soon as Houston woke us. No time for coffee or anything, just, "Begin maneuvers." The Extra-Vehicular Mobility Unit—the spacesuit—was difficult to manage on earth; here, with no gravity, it's incredibly tough. The suits were mounted on the wall of the airlock, where Rob and Darlene helped us put them on. The torso is hard, like a turtle's carapace; the bottom is soft and flexible, so we can move a little bit, at least. The helmets came next, locking onto the neck ring. We put our backpacks on and started to breathe pure oxygen in preparation for our ascent from the pressurized cabin. Finally, the gloves went on and locked in place on the arms. Looking like two creatures from the black lagoon, we waved good-bye to our friends and climbed through the locks into the payload bay, where our module awaited us.

The unit is small, and as much as we practiced in it on Earth with the suits on, here we kept bumping into each other as we got into position for the launch. I tried to make some minor trajectory adjustments before deployment, and Dean was impatient with me, insisting that I was wasting valuable time. Jeff didn't seem to think so; he ended up asking Dean to do the same just before liftoff, which was at 28.52 hours, day two — just barely — of our three weeks.

I must confess that I was terrified when we got down to ejection from the *Liberator*. My colleagues, their cameras at the ready, took a lot of long shots of me alone—for the media, of course. What was Dean feeling then? Mr. Perfection, always in control, ready for any maneuver, seemed so cool, as if he did this every day. I have this strange feeling that he's a bit miffed at being the man behind the scenes, that I'm going to get all the glory for this "solo" expedition. Am I reading that in? As well as I think I know him, I still find moments when we seem distant, separate. I guess there's nothing wrong with that, and yet I miss him then.

"What are you writing?" Dean looked over at Jennie, strapped to her couch, holding a pencil in the air.

"Just some notes," she said matter-of-factly. I was writing about you, you dolt, and how much I love you, even when you act as if you have to be in charge or the world may blow up, she thought. "Ready to get started on some of my experiments?" Hastily, she put the diary away.

"I've got some important things to do first, Jennie. I want to secure the module for any hydrogen or oxygen leaks, check temperatures—that sort of thing. You can set up the testing apparatus, but I'll be busy here for a while."

She looked at him. "Why don't you let me do the fuel and oxygen checks? That's what I was trained for."

"No, I'd rather see to it myself. Dying for a cup of coffee, though. Want one?"

"I'd love one. Give me a call when it's ready."

He shook his head and buried himself in his manual. "I thought you might take care of that."

She almost laughed. On earth, he never would have expected her to fetch and carry. "Dean, what is this? I'm not along for the ride, you know. This is a partnership."

He turned to face her, his angular face looking even more etched in the neon lights. "Why so touchy, sweetheart? All I said was I had some things to do. You don't seem to be particularly swamped right now, so I figured—"

"You figured coffee was easy. Any woman could do it."

"Jennie!" He whirled around, then floated over to her, grabbing her by one arm. "If you so much as dare to imply that I don't think your work is as important as mine . . ."

"Yeah? Well, do you?"

"There is a time and a place for everything." He looked longingly at the panel full of circuit breakers he'd been studying. The tiny module in which they were now orbiting alone was a shuttle in miniature, but it seemed to have just as many switches, toggles, levers, and rods as the larger craft—no pilot worth his salt could keep his hands off them. "So," he finished, realizing he was being competitive and difficult, "I guess this time I'll do the coffee."

He made his way over to the kitchen area as she looked at him, puzzled, saying nothing. She watched him take out two bags of the dehydrated mixture, one with sugar and cream, one with cream only, and attach them to the hot-water spigot. Then he kneaded each one carefully, mixing the processed ingredients until they dissolved. A check valve on the bag prevented the hot liquid from escaping, and a tube on the opposite end was used for sucking. He took the two containers and glided back, presenting her with one.

"Thanks." She took it and started to suck on the tube, then stopped. "This is awful."

"Wait till lunch. I hear the cream-of-chicken soup is better. Rates four spoons." He was mad at himself and at her, furious that they were already so edgy with each other.

He put the bag down and looked at her, reaching for one floating hand. "Hey, why are we doing this to each other?"

"Because we don't agree on the merits of your work as opposed to my work. I thought it was all *our* work. So stop patronizing me, Dean."

He looked up, surprised. "Sweetheart, we're going to be here for a while. You'll have plenty of opportunity to do what you're supposed to—"

"And so will you." She shook her head. "Whew! Talk about a tension-filled three weeks. This is tough. I guess I thought about it when Peter told me we'd be assigned together, but I had no idea what it might really be like. Just . . . just don't jump down my throat about what's vital and what can wait. You have the technical matters to deal with; I have the scientific end. And then," she added shyly, "we have each other."

"You're not kidding." He left his tube hanging in space and turned her to him slowly. They hung there together for a while, not needing to be any closer. Then he reached for her, drawing her body across the light space that separated them. Their lips met gently.

It was a delicious sensation, like being awakened from a long, refreshing nap. Jennie moved her mouth just slightly, and that separated them. She felt her breathing heighten, and it became perfectly clear to her that proximity to this man in a working situation was going to be increasingly difficult. They had so much to get done, so little time to do it. And he still had the uncanny ability to make her mind and heart do somersaults whenever she was with him. She couldn't risk wrecking her work for the sake of these giddy, out-of-control feelings. This was the biggest opportunity of her life—and in the back of her mind, she still worried that the least little distraction might cause her to botch it up. Since Dean was a monumental distraction, her only course of action was to pretend there was nothing between them, impossible as that might seem.

"Listen, what do you say we cool it with each other while we're here? I mean, the strain of being guinea pigs together is only going to get worse." As soon as the practical words were out of her mouth, she hated herself for ever suggesting such a thing. Whenever the hardnosed scientist rose to the surface, Jennie got pushed underwater.

"I think . . . I think that's a very good idea," he lied. What was the matter with her? Just feeling her body brush against his in the tight confines of their module made him long for her. He wanted to crush her to him, damn gravity, full steam ahead. But he did respect her wishes. He was too much in love with her not to. "So no frivolity, no hanky-panky. Nothing more exciting than a rousing game of space checkers at night. How's that?"

She looked into his midnight eyes, unable to tell whether he was serious or just humoring her. To be perfectly honest, she had hoped that he would disagree, that he would take her into his arms and strip off her jumpsuit in a rage of passion. How absurd, Jennie, she told herself, floating over to her box of equipment. He's a professional, just as you are.

They talked to the shuttle once that afternoon and corrected their course slightly. The two crafts were in orbit about fifteen miles apart, but only rarely could they spot one another out the windows. Darlene confirmed that everyone missed them; Rob made a few off-color jokes; Jeff and James reported that, although they'd gotten all their meals down, they were still experiencing a little queasiness. Jennie advised them to keep their heads as still as possible, so as not to disturb the fluid of their inner ears. She also suggested they take the mild anti-nauseant NASA always provided on board. To tell the truth, she wasn't feeling so well herself—not that she'd let on to them *or* Dean. They sent regards to Houston, then signed off.

In the afternoon, they got down to business and started slowly on the experiments. Her plan was to work up gradually, stressing their bodies more each day as the weightlessness took its toll on their various organs. She set up the treadmill and started unpacking her biomedical sensors.

"I want four of these taped across your chest, like so," she said, demonstrating on her own slim body. "Two on your head, two each on the arms and legs. And one here." She pointed toward his groin area.

He grinned at her lasciviously. "You'd better do it; I might hit the wrong spot."

"No, thanks. I don't want temptation standing in my path."

"Well, sweetheart," he said, peeling down to his shorts in weightless slow motion, "you haven't got a choice. Standing is what temptation always does when you're around."

She couldn't look at him as he hooked himself up, so

she concentrated on her statistics instead. She kept reviewing the information as she strapped him to the treadmill and began his stress tests. It was all stuff she knew like she knew the alphabet, but she found herself unable to concentrate on her work. He was so present before her, a massive force that threatened to knock over all her good intentions. What was worse, he appeared to be completely aware of the effect he was having on her—and to be enjoying the hell out of it.

"Blood pressure is one hundred thirty-five over one hundred two at maximum," she reported half an hour later. "Pulse is ninety-six, and you're not even sweating."

"I know something that'll raise my blood pressure. Yours, too."

She swallowed hard, then released the treadmill lever to a more comfortable level so that he could walk instead of jog in place. "All right, that's enough for today. I want to work on the isometrics tomorrow. You can take a rest and clock me."

"Be my pleasure. What else do you have up your sleeve for the next three weeks?" He grabbed her hand, which had just reached for the straps that held him secure to the treadmill.

"Oh, Lord, Dean, don't make it harder for us!" She gasped as he took her in his arms, pulling her down to his level on the floor.

"Why are you fighting this?" he whispered, stirring her tousled auburn curls with his hot breath.

She was filled with an aching desire for him, and as his leg brushed hers and he floated free of the apparatus, she knew there was no turning back. Their mouths met, opening to welcome each sweet embrace. Over on one end, they collided with a side of the module, and she pushed off into his strong, warm body. His hands were all over her now, stroking her and fueling the fires that she had tried to quench. He tumbled down to the level of her breasts and wrapped his muscular arms around her. Then, together, they glided, spinning endlessly in one small space, spinning into each other's hearts and minds.

The zipper of her jumpsuit felt cold against her bare flesh as he effortlessly pulled it down, holding her against the wall for leverage. His eyes opened wide when he saw that she was wearing nothing underneath.

"I figured it would be easier to take sponge baths this way." She shrugged, floating back toward him and reaching for his shorts.

"I think that's very wise. You're very clever. Oh, Jennie, I never knew it would hurt to love someone this much. But it's a good kind of hurting." He wrapped his legs around hers, holding her to him with a fierce determination that spoke of desire and caring and gentleness. "I never knew it felt like this."

Naked together, like the first man and woman, they circled the space in a feather-light erotic dance that took them head over heels into positions no one had ever dreamed of back on earth. Now she was a butterfly on his shoulders, now a waistband that enveloped him in warm curves and rounded breasts. He became her pillar of strength, tossing her easily into the air like an expert juggler, happy in his work. Their hands and mouths were always busy, slowly drawing the most intense and passionate responses from one another.

He took one rosy nipple in his mouth, and it arched eagerly toward him. Then she offered him the other, and he lapped at it while reaching lower for the prize he knew she would never deny him. But as soon as he released her back, she floated away, an elusive spirit even gravity couldn't have tamed. When she lunged for him, she grabbed air, and even his beckoning manhood seemed to drift from her. Like two brave bullfighters, they passed again and again, crossing limbs and futilely diving for the one form of union that would bring them closer than they had ever been.

The fact that they wanted each other so badly and

couldn't consummate their passion made them both a little crazy. Jennie felt herself roused to a state she had no control over, and there was no turning back from this pinnacle of desire. This was space rapture indeed, the heady yearning that fogged the mind and made every other gesture, every other sight and sound, meaningless.

Dean groaned deep in his chest and lunged for her again, pinioning her against one of the bulkheads. He grabbed behind him and linked his arm through a strap, then secured his foot through one of the footrests. Thus anchored, he was able to lavish all his expert attention on the body of his beloved, her beautiful need for him making her all the more desirable. He kissed her shoulders, then made his way down to her flat stomach, pausing lightly to run his tongue around her nipples once again. She tried to move against him, tried to press herself closer, but only his tight embrace made a difference now. She heard her voice coming from far away, calling for him, begging for him to enter her and bring this exhilaration to its peak.

But still he refused, demanding time to work her to the limits of her sanity. He released her slightly, which brought her body floating higher in his grasp. He mouthed the soft auburn curls below and then parted her legs masterfully but delicately so that he could touch the soft, spun-silk skin of her inner thighs. She was in a frenzy now, unable to stop the sounds that made him know it was time. It was their time.

He held her buttocks, and, with a firm grip on the strap, he entered her swiftly and easily. He let her move around him, causing him such a sudden edge of pleasure that he nearly let her go. But something beyond him made him hold on for dear life, made him twine his legs through hers and let her rhythm carry them both. They hung suspended in space, trusting their instincts, and with Dean as the brace, they worked their way upward, toward a climax that seemed endless, a joyful ride into their own future.

Jennie's mouth opened in a wide O, and she exploded with the fullness of her love for him. Never had she imagined that passion and tenderness and the excitement of being close could ever move her this way. Then she heard him answer her cries and felt them float free as he abandoned their little life raft and allowed them to spin loosely around the cabin. There was no resistance, no pressure, hardly any feeling of movement at all. But she still felt him inside her, and that made her glow once again as they tumbled over and over, daring the elements to overtake them and separate them. But together they remained, their lips murmuring the sweetest words ever spoken, their hands still linked, their hearts pounding with excitement.

As they lay quietly in the air, the sunlight rushed away from the windows, leaving only the crisp autumn fire of crimson and mauve, which burnished their two bodies with its colorful brilliance. They both turned to it, smiling, and Dean brushed a loose strand of hair from her face so he could see her better. This slight gesture finally parted them, and they gently moved away from each other, clutching hands to keep their contact.

"Some sunset." Dean grinned, indicating the light show outside the window.

"Completely and utterly wonderful," Jennie concurred, but she wasn't referring to the play of light and darkness outside.

"Dr. Jacobs, I think we've just made history," Dean told her, reaching out to bring them back together again. He looked down, suddenly realizing that he was still wearing the biomedical sensors. "I have a feeling the numbers went off your charts, though. Now, as a bona fide scientist, I guess you'd better take some readings."

She shook her head. "Not on your life, Dean! What would NASA say when I explained what they were readings for?"

He rubbed his broad forehead studiously. "How about calling it 'Emotional Survival Techniques in Space'? That sounds like something they'd approve of."

"Hey, you know..." She started laughing. "I can't believe this, but it's absolutely true. I didn't tell you, but I was a little nauseated ever since we lifted off from the shuttle. But it's gone now—not a trace of it. So I was right! I said it was just like jet lag, and sex takes care of jet lag. Genius!"

"It takes care of more than that." Dean's voice grew soft, and as he drew her to one of the forward windows, there was a misty look in his eyes. "You've done something to me, Jennie. You've made me a person, not just a functioning machine. You've brought daylight into my life." There were tears in his eyes as he pointed out to the field of stars that glistened before them in their very own private universe. "It makes you feel so small, doesn't it? Such a speck in the great scheme of things."

"Yes, but it makes me proud, too," she answered, her eyes filling as she peered into the void. "We're part of it. We always will be."

The great dark wash of sky was testimony to their love, holding them tight, feeding and nourishing them as a mother does her children. In the vast quiet of space, they lay still, communicating silently and peacefully until, a few minutes later, the sun rushed back at them, demanding their attention.

"I know this sounds ridiculous, but we're supposed to talk to Houston sometime today. Want to put your clothes on?" Dean winked at her, but it took him a while because gravity wasn't there to help pull down on his eye muscles.

"No, not particularly, but we can't make an appearance on TV in the buff. What do we tell them?" she asked innocently.

"I think we should notify them that compatibility is at maximum," Dean said decisively, depositing a kiss on her departing back, "and that if they want us to stay up for a year, we'd consider it."

Giggling and bumping each other playfully, they dove

for their floating clothes and quickly suited up again. When they were ready at last to reestablish contact, it was with total sobriety that they peered into the TV camera and flipped the switch.

"Houston, do you read?" Dean called into the communicator.

"We have you in view, *Specialist*," Abby said, using the name NASA had given to the module once it was free of the shuttle. "How are things going?"

Jennie took a deep breath and responded, "Tests are progressing fine, thanks. Neither of us is wild about the food, but I'm happy to report absolutely no disorientation or nausea for either of us."

Abby gave a low whistle into the mike. "You guys are lucky. Apparently the shuttle crew is a mess this afternoon. What's your secret?"

Dean swallowed a laugh and peered at Jennie with a completely straight face. "Dr. Jacobs's magic elixir. Remind us to tell you about it when we're debriefed."

"You bet I will. Peter and Ann want to know if you have any problems at all. Three weeks is a long time together, twenty-four hours a day."

Dean grabbed Jennie's hand under the console. "Not for us," he told mission control. "Because we've got the right stuff."

And when they signed off a few minutes later and Dean took Jennie in his arms, she looked up at him with shining eyes, realizing that her life had started again. No longer confined by her own doubts and misgivings, she had been freed to face her desires and hopes head on and open her heart to a man who offered her the challenge of a new world, one that would be shared completely. There, riding high on top of the moon and stars, they pledged silently and solemnly their extraordinary love.

- 13 -

"COULD WE HAVE just one more, Jennie? Right profile this time."

"Turn this way! Over here, Jen. What was it like, being alone in space for three weeks? Can you give us any insight into what your feelings were?"

"How did the experiments go? Have you solved the motion sickness problem?"

"Jennie! Dr. Jacobs! Look this way!"

Jennie was blinded by one flashbulb after another. She'd never seen so many reporters in one gaggle before, and it was more disorienting than any physical sensations she'd had in space. The crowd was too rowdy, too eager for her. She smiled and babbled some nonsense about major breakthroughs in her field, looking helplessly at Dan Abrams, her PR director, and at Peter Reinhardt. They might have rescued her from the barrage of insistent questions, but they were busy fending off even more reporters.

Since Jeff had brought them in for a perfect landing at Edwards Air Force Base an hour ago, she'd been the sole focus of attention. The rest of the crew, including

Dean, stood behind her and watched as Jennie got the brunt of it.

"That's enough now. These astronauts have to get some rest and a shower," Peter said at last. "Then they'll be flying back to Houston for debriefing, so you guys will just have to wait a while." He displayed his best military manner as he grasped Jennie firmly by one arm, steering her out of the mainstream. Dan ushered her colleagues right after. "Whew!" Peter whispered to her conspiratorially as they marched in sloppy formation to the administration building. "We're going to have you on the lecture circuit for months. Hope you like fried chicken."

"As long as I don't have to mix it with hot water and suck it through a tube," she joked good-naturedly.

"So, tell me." His eyes were sparkling. "How was it, really? Can a couple survive up there?"

"Depends on the couple," she answered slyly. "We did fine, Peter," she added when he looked disappointed by her facile answer. "And my test results are astounding. Particularly Dean's. I don't think you'll find any major calcium loss or fluid imbalance. We worked his stress routines so carefully, he hardly knew he wasn't grounded by gravity."

"Yes, yes." Peter nodded impatiently, showing her into the small set of dressing rooms they'd reserved for the astronauts. "I'm thrilled about your work, of course, Jen, but I want to know more. What about the, uh, the psychological ramifications? What about the round-the-clock proximity? Was it..." He paused, obviously choosing his words carefully. "Was it all right?"

Jennie laughed and nodded. "It was all right. Listen, are we ever going to blow the cover on this mission? Will the public ever be informed that I wasn't up there alone?"

Peter harrumphed and looked at his shoes. "Not for me to say. I think it'll depend on later developments. We don't want to leave too much to the people's imagination, Jennie. You can pretty well figure out what they might think."

She rolled her eyes, feigning innocence. "Why, Peter, I'm shocked." She grinned.

"As I said before," he grunted, "you're the wackiest girl we've got in the program. I mean, just because you can tolerate being alone with a man, day after day, moment after moment, for weeks at a stretch doesn't mean it'll seem that simple to the media. But the question remains," he said, stolidly returning to his point, "can we set up a space station and be certain of a small crew's emotional stability for six months or more? That's the meat of it."

Jennie paused, watching Dean wink at her broadly and then disappear behind a door to the showers. "I think I can safely say, Peter," she began with a completely emotionless expression on her face, "that this particular voyage was exceptionally successful. You'll have to try it again, naturally, with other teams. But ours"—she smiled gently—"was a winner."

If anything, the three weeks had passed too swiftly for Dean and Jennie. The module maintenance and weightlessness tests had taken up a good part of each day, but the endless evenings of star-gazing and love-making had been the culmination. Oh, they still fought occasionally about who was supposed to do what when— but then, they were competitive people. That would never change. They learned, over the weeks, which buttons the other person couldn't stand to have pushed. And they learned, simply, how to love more deeply. Their isolation gave them the uninterrupted time to open up their souls to each other.

They docked with the shuttle on the twenty-first day at zero-six hundred hours, only to find a very bored, very restless crew. Darlene was dying for a shower, Rob wouldn't stop talking about food, James still wasn't feeling well, and Jeff was just barely managing to keep the group from mass mutiny. They seemed glad to have Dean and Jennie back.

Returning to earth was perhaps more spectacular than leaving it. They could feel the deceleration happening, and see it, too. As they zoomed down through the upper atmosphere, the sky went crazy. The blackness of space gave way to an incredible circle of lavender, blue-green, and some violet, surrounding a central yellow-orange core. Recaptured by the earth's atmosphere, the shuttle plummeted downward, and pretty soon Jennie felt the pressure of 6.5 G's sitting right on her chest. It didn't matter, though, how hard life pressed on her now. She looked over at Dean, and he flashed her a look of adoration so tender, so giving, that she was instantly calmed. They were going home.

What would it be like, now that they were back on their own territory? she wondered as she escaped from the group, claiming that she had to have a shower or she'd flake apart.

She let the streams of steamy water soak out the tension in her shoulders. She scrubbed her hair, then each limb, relishing the smooth passage of the bar of clean-smelling soap on her body. Like Dean's hands, she thought, closing her eyes briefly. It was so nice in here, so pleasant. It would be so easy just to relax and fall asleep.

She jerked to attention, remembering at the penultimate moment that fainting in a hot shower was one of the most common occurrences after a long space flight. You didn't use your legs in space, so when you returned to gravity, your blood rushed back to pool in the lower extremities, which in turn robbed the head and torso of its usual supply. She gasped as she switched the shower knob to cold, feeling her skin retract from the extreme temperature. Be tough, kid, she told herself as she stoically shut her eyes to the blast.

There were fresh jumpsuits waiting for all of them and a not particularly sumptuous meal of tuna fish sandwiches and orange juice. But they gobbled their food dutifully. By 2:00 P.M. they were ready to board the plane back to Houston for their debriefing.

Their arrival on the airfield was heralded by another crazed horde of reporters and well-wishers. No sooner had they stepped outside than they heard the cheers of the mob. Autograph hounds waved their pencils and paper frantically; fathers lifted little children on their shoulders to see the conquering heroes.

"You get in the middle," Dean insisted, pushing Jennie in front of him, between Rob and Jeff. "Let's see if we can take off some of the heat."

She looked at him gratefully, realizing how difficult this must be for him. He loved the limelight and wouldn't get to bask in its warmth at all. He could tolerate that only because he loved her—and respected her as an accomplished astronaut.

"Fat chance," Darlene replied. "She's the Michael Jackson of astronauts right now."

Dean ignored this comment and tried to field a few questions. "Dr. Jacobs is a little tired right now, so if there's anything you want to know," he said genially, surreptitiously running his hand down her bare right forearm, "I'd be happy to try to answer your questions."

Aside from the women ogling his impressive physique, nobody paid much attention to him.

"Dr. Jacobs," one reporter bellowed, "give us some dope on the support crew. Did the rest of these guys give you the help you needed?"

"Hey, they were just as vital to this mission as I was," she told the man hotly. "If it hadn't been for them..." she began, but her voice, hoarse from calling out dozens of responses, cracked in mid-sentence. Then she turned to Dean, a pleading look in her eyes.

"If it hadn't been for us," Dean began, a cagey smile

playing around his full mouth, "she would have been awfully lonely."

"Jennie, c'mon, answer a few more!" somebody called.

Dean pushed her up the staircase and into the small plane, and the others rushed in after him. "They're like carpenter ants. Swarming all over and hungry as sin," he chuckled. Only Jennie could tell there was a slight edge to his humor. Nobody wanted to talk to him. Mr. Perfection, the ace flyer, the top of his class! He was trying so hard not to let the hurt show—and all for her!

She could see him holding his pride in check, trying to let her have her glory and not compete. It was probably one of the hardest things he'd ever done—certainly more difficult than flying a jet upside down at Mach 1.

"You were swell out there," she whispered to him when they were finally strapped into their seats and the pilot informed them that they were ready for takeoff.

"No, I wasn't. Didn't do a thing for you."

"It's the thought that counts. Did Peter tell you about the party tonight?" she added when he didn't respond.

"Oh, no. Not one of those hold-your-cocktail-and-smile affairs." He sighed wearily. "I'm no good at those."

"Darling, I have this dynamite dress I've never worn— all burgundy sparkles and very low cut. You aren't going to do me out of wearing that!" Jennie said indignantly.

He looked at her face, then let his eyes roam to other parts of her anatomy. "You know, I've never seen you in a dress."

"You'll like it." She was blushing at his insistent attention. Even now, after all this intimate time together, he still had the power to fluster her totally.

"I like you best without any kind of clothes at all," he admitted. "But I'm willing to give it a try. Too bad we have to go to Peter's party, though. I'd hoped we might have our own," he whispered.

"That comes later. After the dress comes off." There was promise in her voice and in her eyes as she spoke.

He wanted nothing more than to get her alone again, for hours—days if possible. Flight together had been wonderful, of course, but he needed the feel of her body against his, the hard impact of gravity drawing them back together. Now he knew what he wanted, and he wouldn't stop until he had all of it, all of her. As the afternoon and the debriefing progressed, he couldn't think of anything else. The words he wanted to say to her were scorching his mouth, ripping a searing path right through him.

They stopped at his place so that he could pick up his dress khakis and then went on to Jennie's house. Wings was waiting in the window for them, and gave them such a yowl of indignity and displeasure as they walked into the house that they nearly turned around and left again.

"She's furious! I've never left her this long before," Jennie moaned, picking up the hissing cat and stroking her back into submission.

"I thought cats were supposed to be independent," Dean said, ruffling her hair and trying to draw her away from the animal.

"Don't you believe it! They need us as much as we need them. Just like some people I could mention." They linked hands and wandered over to her beloved Oriental rug, where he pulled her down beside him. They'd been with people nonstop for nearly twenty-four hours now, and their need for each other was almost palpable.

"Let's skip the party," he murmured, pushing her slightly off balance so that she lay back on the rug, her lovely curls a profusion of fire on the mingled rose-and-blue weave. "You can wear the dress here—for a while."

"Illegal! No way, José! You realize how many demerits we'd get for that? And Peter would break down and cry." She gave him a disparaging glance and got to her feet. "I'll get us some tea. It'll bring you to your senses."

"I don't want to come to my senses. Not ever." He

grabbed onto her ankle and dragged her back down, making her squeal for mercy as she landed on top of him. His mouth covered hers greedily, hungrily. She was pliant and yielding, granting him all he wanted from her.

"I have to tell you something," he said quietly when at last they came up for air. "A long time ago, before I knew you, I dreamed about you. You hauled me in from the black void of space single-handed. No mechanical difficulties, no fuss. For you, it was easy."

She sat up, smiling. "Oh, it was, was it? Now what would Freud say about that?"

"He would undoubtedly say"—Dean held her tightly, and his voice softened to a gentle rumble—"that I've loved you for a long time. That I was waiting all my life for you. That my damned competitive attitude and my shyness kept me away for a while, but now I'm here for you forever. Which is a good thing, because when you're about to perform the all-important ETBM maneuver, you have to be together."

She frowned suspiciously and squirmed around in his arms. "ETBM? That's an acronym I must have forgotten."

"Engaged to be married, you sweet dope. We are, aren't we?"

She felt a lump in her throat as she nodded blindly, knowing that this was exactly where their lives had been leading them, feeling secure in his arms and in his love.

He drew her up, and they walked to the window together, just in time for the last sunset of their long day. It was spectacular, a panoply of fire that matched the flames glowing brightly in their hearts.

"You may have that baby on the moon after all," he said when the last traces of gold and red had left the sky. "We'll time the shoot for it. That's after we've scored with the first anti-gravity wedding."

She nodded. "Peter would love it. Great publicity." She took his rugged face in her hands and stroked his cheek gently. "I never knew I could feel this way," she said. "And yet, it's so natural to me now. It's natural to love you."

He looked at her softly, his dark blue eyes absorbing her beauty and her complete trust in him. "God, Jennie, if the world could be as happy as we are now, we wouldn't have to fly to distant planets. We wouldn't have to worry about wasting this one. We'd all have our feet on the ground at every moment."

"Uh-uh," she chided him gently. "We'd all be flying. Just like you and me. Never let me land, baby. This is where I want to be."

He held her close, and darkness enveloped them as their love grew to a white-hot flame within. Just before their lips met to meld them together, a shooting star cascaded down from the heavens, from the place they'd just left. They both smiled in awe; the magical sky and the heavens seemed to be giving their blessing to the two lovers.

A new constellation was born for Jennie and Dean that wonderful night. It was a symbol of eternity, of love and peace, and it would belong to them, completely and utterly, forever and ever.

Second Chance at Love ®

___ 0-425-07773-X	INTRUDER'S KISS #246 Carole Buck	$2.25
___ 0-425-07774-8	LADY BE GOOD #247 Elissa Curry	$2.25
___ 0-425-07775-6	A CLASH OF WILLS #248 Lauren Fox	$2.25
___ 0-425-07776-4	SWEPT AWAY #249 Jacqueline Topaz	$2.25
___ 0-425-07975-9	PAGAN HEART #250 Francine Rivers	$2.25
___ 0-425-07976-7	WORDS OF ENDEARMENT #251 Helen Carter	$2.25
___ 0-425-07977-5	BRIEF ENCOUNTER #252 Aimée Duvall	$2.25
___ 0-425-07978-3	FOREVER EDEN #253 Christa Merlin	$2.25
___ 0-425-07979-1	STARDUST MELODY #254 Mary Haskell	$2.25
___ 0-425-07980-5	HEAVEN TO KISS #255 Charlotte Hines	$2.25
___ 0-425-08014-5	AIN'T MISBEHAVING #256 Jeanne Grant	$2.25
___ 0-425-08015-3	PROMISE ME RAINBOWS #257 Joan Lancaster	$2.25
___ 0-425-08016-1	RITES OF PASSION #258 Jacqueline Topaz	$2.25
___ 0-425-08017-X	ONE IN A MILLION #259 Lee Williams	$2.25
___ 0-425-08018-8	HEART OF GOLD #260 Liz Grady	$2.25
___ 0-425-08019-6	AT LONG LAST LOVE #261 Carole Buck	$2.25
___ 0-425-08150-8	EYE OF THE BEHOLDER #262 Kay Robbins	$2.25
___ 0-425-08151-6	GENTLEMAN AT HEART #263 Elissa Curry	$2.25
___ 0-425-08152-4	BY LOVE POSSESSED #264 Linda Barlow	$2.25
___ 0-425-08153-2	WILDFIRE #265 Kelly Adams	$2.25
___ 0-425-08154-0	PASSION'S DANCE #266 Lauren Fox	$2.25
___ 0-425-08155-9	VENETIAN SUNRISE #267 Kate Nevins	$2.25
___ 0-425-08199-0	THE STEELE TRAP #268 Betsy Osborne	$2.25
___ 0-425-08200-8	LOVE PLAY #269 Carole Buck	$2.25
___ 0-425-08201-6	CAN'T SAY NO #270 Jeanne Grant	$2.25
___ 0-425-08202-4	A LITTLE NIGHT MUSIC #271 Lee Williams	$2.25
___ 0-425-08203-2	A BIT OF DARING #272 Mary Haskell	$2.25
___ 0-425-08204-0	THIEF OF HEARTS #273 Jan Mathews	$2.25
___ 0-425-08284-9	MASTER TOUCH #274 Jasmine Craig	$2.25
___ 0-425-08285-7	NIGHT OF A THOUSAND STARS #275 Petra Diamond	$2.25
___ 0-425-08286-5	UNDERCOVER KISSES #276 Laine Allen	$2.25
___ 0-425-08287-3	MAN TROUBLE #277 Elizabeth Henry	$2.25
___ 0-425-08288-1	SUDDENLY THAT SUMMER #278 Jennifer Rose	$2.25
___ 0-425-08289-X	SWEET ENCHANTMENT #279 Diana Mars	$2.25

Prices may be slightly higher in Canada.

COMING NEXT MONTH
IN THE
SECOND CHANCE AT LOVE SERIES

QUESTIONNAIRE

1. How do you rate _____
                        (please print TITLE)
   ☐ excellent   ☐ good
   ☐ very good   ☐ fair   ☐ poor

2. How likely are you to purchase another book in this series?
   ☐ definitely would purchase
   ☐ probably would purchase
   ☐ probably would not purchase
   ☐ definitely would not purchase

3. How likely are you to purchase another book by this author?
   ☐ definitely would purchase
   ☐ probably would purchase
   ☐ probably would not purchase
   ☐ definitely would not purchase

4. How does this book compare to books in other contemporary romance lines?
   ☐ much better
   ☐ better
   ☐ about the same
   ☐ not as good
   ☐ definitely not as good

5. Why did you buy this book? (Check as many as apply)
   ☐ I have read other
      SECOND CHANCE AT LOVE romances
   ☐ friend's recommendation
   ☐ bookseller's recommendation
   ☐ art on the front cover
   ☐ description of the plot on the back cover
   ☐ book review I read
   ☐ other _____
           _____
           _____

(Continued...)

6. Please list your three favorite contemporary romance lines.

_____
_____

7. Please list your favorite authors of contemporary romance lines.

_____
_____
_____
_____
_____
_____

8. How many SECOND CHANCE AT LOVE romances have you read? _____

9. How many series romances like SECOND CHANCE AT LOVE do you <u>read</u> each month? _____

10. How many series romances like SECOND CHANCE AT LOVE do you <u>buy</u> each month? _____

11. Mind telling your age?
☐ under 18
☐ 18 to 30
☐ 31 to 45
☐ over 45

☐ Please check if you'd like to receive our <u>free</u> SECOND CHANCE AT LOVE Newsletter.

We hope you'll share your other ideas about romances with us on an additional sheet and attach it securely to this questionnaire.

• •

Fill in your name and address below:
Name _____
Street Address _____
City _____ State _____ Zip _____

Please return this questionnaire to:
SECOND CHANCE AT LOVE
The Berkley Publishing Group
200 Madison Avenue, New York, New York 10016